I0764563

The Man in Grey
&
In the Rue Monge

by
Baroness Emma Orczy

Printed on acid free ANSI archival quality paper.

Contents

The Man in Grey

PROEM

IT has been a difficult task to piece together the fragmentary documents which alone throw a light--dim and flickering at the best--upon that mysterious personality known to the historians of the Napoleonic era as the Man in Grey. So very little is known about him. Age, appearance, domestic circumstances, everything pertaining to him has remained a matter of conjecture--even his name! In the reports sent by the all-powerful Minister to the Emperor he is invariably spoken of as "The Man in Grey." Once only does Fouché refer to him as "Fernand."

Strange and mysterious creature! Nevertheless, he played an important part--the most important, perhaps in bringing to justice some of those reckless criminals who, under the cloak of Royalist convictions and religious and political aims, spent their time in pillage, murder and arson.

Strange and mysterious creatures, too, these men so aptly named Chouans--that is, "chats-huants"; screech-owls--since they were a terror by night and disappeared within their burrows by day. A world of romance lies buried within the ruins of the châteaux which gave them shelter--Tournebut, Bouvesse, Donnai, Plélan. A world of mystery encompasses the names of their leaders and, above all, those of the women--ladies of high degree and humble peasants alike--often heroic, more often misguided, who supplied the intrigue, the persistence, the fanatical hatred which kept the fire of rebellion smouldering and spluttering even while it could not burst into actual flame. D'Aché Cadoudal, Frotté, Armand le Chevallier, Marquise de Combray, Mme. Aquet de Férolles--the romance attaching to these names pales beside that which clings to the weird anonymity of their henchmen--"Dare-Death," "Hare-Lip," "Fear-Nought," "Silver-Leg," and so on. Theirs were the hands that struck whilst their leaders planned--they were the screech-owls who for more than twenty years terrorised the western provinces of France and, in the name of God and their King, committed every crime that could besmirch the Cause which they professed to uphold.

Whether they really aimed at the restoration of the Bourbon kings and at bolstering up the fortunes of an effete and dispossessed monarchy with money wrung from peaceable citizens, or whether they were a mere pack of lawless brigands made up of deserters from the army and fugitives from conscription, of felons and bankrupt aristocrats, will for ever remain a bone of contention between the apologists of the old régime and those of the new.

With partisanship in those strangely obscure though comparatively recent episodes of history we have nothing to do. Facts alone--undeniable and undenied--must be left to speak for themselves. It was but meet that these men--amongst whom were to be found the bearers of some of the noblest names in France--should be tracked down and brought to justice by one whose personality has continued to be as complete an enigma as their own.

I. SILVER-LEG

I

"FORWARD now! And at foot-pace, mind, to the edge of the wood--or----"

The ominous click of a pistol completed the peremptory command.

Old Gontran, the driver, shook his wide shoulders beneath his heavy caped coat and gathered the reins once more in his quivering hands; the door of the coach was closed with a bang; the postilion scrambled into the saddle; only the passenger who had so peremptorily been ordered down from the box-seat beside the driver had not yet climbed back into his place. Well! old Gontran was not in a mood to fash about the passengers. His horses, worried by the noise, the shouting, the click of firearms and the rough handling meted out to them by strange hands in the darkness, were very restive. They would have liked to start off at once at a brisk pace so as to leave these disturbers of their peace as far behind them as possible, but Gontran was holding them in with a firm hand and they had to walk--walk!--along this level bit of road, with the noisy enemy still present in their rear.

The rickety old coach gave a lurch and started on its way; the clanking of loose chains, the grinding of the wheels in the muddy roads, the snorting and travail of the horses as they finally settled again into their collars, drowned the coachman's muttered imprecations.

"A fine state of things, forsooth!" he growled to himself more dejectedly than savagely. "What the Emperor's police are up to no one knows. That such things can happen is past belief. Not yet six o'clock in the afternoon, and Alençon less than five kilométres in front of us."

But the passenger who, on the box-seat beside him, had so patiently and silently listened to old Gontran's florid loquacity during the early part of the journey, was no longer there to hear these well-justified lamentations. No doubt he had taken refuge with his fellow-sufferers down below.

There came no sound from the interior of the coach. In the darkness, the passengers--huddled up against one another, dumb with fright and wearied with excitement--had not yet found vent for their outraged feelings in whispered words or smothered oaths. The coach lumbered on at foot-pace. In the affray the head-light had been broken; the two lanterns that remained lit up fitfully the tall pine trees on either side of the road and gave momentary glimpses of a mysterious, fairy-like world beyond, through the curtain of dead branches and the veil of tiny bare twigs.

Through the fast gathering gloom the circle of light toyed with the haze of damp and steam which rose from the cruppers, of the horses, and issued from their snorting nostrils. From far away came the cry of a screech-owl and the call of some night beasts on the prowl.

Instinctively, as the road widened out towards the edge of the wood, Gontran gave a click with his tongue and the horses broke into a leisurely trot. Immediately from behind, not forty paces to the rear, there came the sharp detonation of a pistol shot. The horses, still quivering from past terrors, were ready to plunge once more, the wheelers stumbled, the leaders reared, and the team would again have been thrown into confusion but for the presence of mind of the driver and the coolness of the postilion.

"Oh! those accursed brigands!" muttered Gontran through his set teeth as soon as order was restored. "That's just to remind us that they are on the watch. Keep the leaders well in hand, Hector," he shouted to the postilion: "don't let them trot till we are well out of the wood."

Though he had sworn copiously and plentifully at first, when one of those outlaws held a pistol to his head whilst the others ransacked the coach of its contents and terrorised the passengers, he seemed inclined to take the matter philosophically now. After all, he himself had lost nothing; he was too wise a man was old Gontran to carry his wages in his breeches pocket these days, when those accursed Chouans robbed, pillaged and plundered rich and poor alike. No! Gontran flattered himself that the rogues had got nothing out of him: he had lost nothing--not even prestige, for it had been a case of twenty to one at the least, and the brigands had been armed to the teeth. Who could blame him that in such circumstances the sixty-two hundred francs, all in small silver and paper money--which the collector of taxes of the Falaise district was sending up to his chief at Alençon--had passed from the boot of the coach into the hands of that clever band of rascals?

Who could blame him? I say. Surely, not the Imperial Government up in Paris who did not know how to protect its citizens from the depredations of such villains, and had not even succeeded in making the high road between Caen and Alençon safe for peaceable travellers.

Inside the coach the passengers were at last giving tongue to their indignation. Highway robbery at six o'clock in the afternoon, and the evening not a very dark one at that! It were monstrous, outrageous, almost incredible, did not the empty pockets and ransacked valises testify to the scandalous fact. M. Fouché, Duc d'Otrante, was drawing a princely salary as Minister of Police, and yet allowed a mail-coach to he held up and pillaged--almost by daylight and within five kilométres, of the county town!

The last half-hour of the eventful journey flew by like magic: there was so much to say that it became impossible to keep count of time. Alençon was reached before everyone had had a chance of saying just what he or she thought of the whole affair, or of consigning M. le Duc: d'Otrante and all his myrmidons to that particular chamber in Hades which was most suitable for their crimes. Outside the "Adam et Ève," where Gontran finally drew rein, there was a gigantic clatter and din as the passengers tumbled out of the coach, and by the dim light of the nearest street lantern tried to disentangle their own belongings from the pile of ransacked valises which the ostlers had unceremoniously tumbled out in a heap upon the cobble stones. Everyone was talking--no one in especial seemed inclined to listen--anecdotes of former outrages committed by the Chouans were bandied to and fro.

Gontran, leaning against the entrance of the inn, a large mug of steaming wine in his hand, watched with philosophic eye his former passengers, struggling with their luggage. One or two of them were going to spend the night at the "Adam et Ève": they had already filed past him into the narrow passage beyond, where they were now deep in an altercation with Gilles Blaise, the proprietor, on the subject of the price and the situation of their rooms; others had homes or friends in the city, and with their broken valises and bundles in their hands could be seen making their way up the narrow main street, still gesticulating excitedly.

"It's a shocking business, friend Gontran," quoth Gilles Blaise as soon as he had settled with the last of his customers. His gruff voice held a distinct note of sarcasm, for he was a powerful fellow and feared neither footpads nor midnight robbers, nor any other species of those satané Chouans. "I wonder you did not make a better fight for it. You had three or four male passengers aboard----"

"What could I do?" retorted Gontran irritably. "I had my horses to attend to, and did it, let me tell you, with the muzzle of a pistol pressing against my temple."

"You didn't see anything of those miscreants?"

"Nothing. That is----"

"What?"

"Just when I was free once more to gather the reins in my hands and the order 'Forward' was given by those impudent rascals, he who had spoken the order stood for a moment below one of my lanterns."

"And you saw him?"

"As plainly as I see you--except his face, for that was hidden by the wide brim of his hat and by a shaggy beard. But there is one thing I should know him by, if the police ever succeeded in laying hands on the rogue."

"What is that?"

"He had only one leg, the other was a wooden one."

Gilles Blaise gave a loud guffaw. He had never heard of a highwayman with a wooden leg before. "The rascal cannot run far if the police ever do get after him," was his final comment on the situation.

Thereupon Gontran suddenly bethought himself of the passenger who had sat on the box-seat beside him until those abominable footpads had ordered the poor man to get out of their way.

"Have you seen anything of him, Hector?" he queried of the postilion.

"Well, now you mention him," replied the young man slowly, "I don't remember that I have."

"He was not among the lot that came out of the coach."

"He certainly was not."

"I thought when he did not get back to his seat beside me, he had lost his nerve and gone inside."

"So did I."

"Well, then?" concluded Gontran.

But the puzzle thus propounded was beyond Hector's powers of solution. He scratched the back of his head by way of trying to extract thence a key to the enigma.

"We must have left him behind," he suggested.

"He would have shouted after us if we had," commented Gontran. "Unless----" he added with graphic significance.

Hector shook himself like a dog who has come out of the water. The terror of those footpads and of those pistols clicking in the dark, unpleasantly close to his head, was still upon him.

"You don't think----" he murmured through chattering teeth.

Gontran shrugged his shoulders.

"It won't be the first time," he said sententiously, "that those miscreants have added murder to their other crimes."

"Lost one of your passengers, Gontran?" queried Gilles Blaise blandly.

"If those rogues have murdered him----" quoth Gontran with an oath.

"Then you'd have to make a special declaration before the chief commissary of police, and that within an hour. Who was your passenger, Gontran?"

"I don't know. A quiet, well-mannered fellow. Good company he was, too, during the first part of the way."

"What was his name?"

"I can't tell. I picked him up at Argentan. The box-seat was empty. No one wanted it, for it was raining then. He paid me his fare and scrambled up beside me. That's all I know about him."

"What was he like? Young or old?"

"I didn't see him very well. It was already getting dark," rejoined Gontran impatiently. "I couldn't look him under the nose, could I?"

"But sacrebleu! Monsieur le Commissaire de Police will want to know something more than that. Did you at least see how he was dressed?"

"Yes," replied Gontran, "as far as I can recollect he was dressed in grey."

"Well, then, friend Gontran," concluded Gilles Blaise with a jovial laugh, "you can go at once to Monsieur le Commissaire de Police, and you can tell him that an industrious Chouan, who has a wooden leg and a shaggy beard but whose face you did not see, has to the best of your belief murdered an unknown passenger whose name, age and appearance you know nothing about, but who, as far as you can recollect, was dressed in grey---- And we'll see," he added with a touch of grim humour, "what Monsieur le Commissaire will make out of this valuable information."

II

The men were cowering together in a burrow constructed of dead branches and caked mud, with a covering of heath and dried twigs. Their heads were close to one another and the dim light of a dark lanthorn placed upon the floor threw weird, sharp shadows across their eager faces, making them appear grotesque and almost ghoulish--the only bright spots in the surrounding gloom.

One man on hands and knees was crouching by the narrow entrance, his keen eyes trying to pierce the density of the forest beyond.

The booty was all there, spread out upon the damp earth--small coins and bundles of notes all smeared with grease and mud; there were some trinkets, too, but of obviously little value: a pair of showy gold earrings, one or two signets, a heavy watch in a chased silver case. But these had been contemptuously swept aside--it was the money that mattered. The man with the wooden leg had counted it all out and was now putting coins and notes back into a large leather wallet.

"Six thousand two hundred and forty-seven francs," he said quietly, as he drew the thongs of the wallet closely together and tied them securely into a knot. "One of the best hauls we've ever had. 'Tis Madame who will be pleased."

"Our share will have to be paid out of that first," commented one of his companions.

"Yes, yes!" quoth the other lightly. "Madame will see to it. She always does. How many of you are there?" he added carelessly.

"Seven of us all told. They were a pack of cowards in that coach."

"Well!" concluded the man with the wooden leg, "we must leave Madame to settle accounts. I'd best place the money in safety now."

He struggled up into a standing position--which was no easy matter for him with his stump and in the restricted space--and was about to hoist the heavy wallet on to his powerful shoulders, when one of his mates seized him by the wrist.

"Hold on, Silver-Leg!" he said roughly, "we'll pay ourselves for our trouble first. Eh, friends?" he added, turning to the others.

But before any of them could reply there came a peremptory command from the man whom they had called "Silver-Leg."

"Silence!" he whispered hoarsely. "There's someone moving out there among the trees."

At once the others obeyed, every other thought lulled to rest by the sense of sudden danger. For a minute or so every sound was hushed in the narrow confines of the lair save the stertorous breathing which came from panting throats. Then the look-out man at the entrance whispered under his breath:

"I heard nothing."

"Something moved, I tell you," rejoined Silver-Leg curtly. "It may only have been a beast on the prowl."

But the brief incident had given him the opportunity which he required; he had shaken off his companion's hold upon his wrist and had slung the wallet over his shoulder. Now he stumped out of the burrow.

"Friend Hare-Lip," he said before he went, in the same commanding tone wherewith he had imposed silence awhile ago on his turbulent mates, "tell Monseigneur that it will be 'Corinne' this time, and you, Mole-Skin, ask Madame to send Red-Poll over on Friday night for the key."

The others growled in assent and followed him out of their hiding-place. One of the men had extinguished the lanthorn, and another was hastily collecting the trinkets which had so contemptuously been swept aside.

"Hold on, Silver-Leg!" shouted the man who had been called Hare-Lip; "short reckonings make long friends. I'll have a couple of hundred francs now," he continued roughly. "It may be days and weeks ere I see Madame again, and by that time God knows where the money will be."

But Silver-Leg stumped on in the gloom, paying no heed to the peremptory calls of his mates. It was marvellous how fast he contrived to hobble along, winding his way in and out in the darkness, among the trees, on the slippery carpet of pine needles and carrying that heavy wallet--six thousand two hundred francs, most of it in small coin--upon his back. The others, however, were swift and determined, too. Within the next minute or two they had overtaken him, and he could no longer evade them; they held him tightly, surrounding him on every side and clamouring for their share of the spoils.

"We'll settle here and now, friend Silver-Leg," said Hare-Lip, who appeared to be the acknowledged spokesman of the malcontents. "Two hundred francs for me out of that wallet, if you please, ere you move another step, and two hundred for each one of us here, or----"

The man with the wooden leg had come to a halt, but somehow it seemed that he had not done so because the others held and compelled him, but because he himself had a desire to stand still. Now when Hare-Lip paused, a world of menace in every line of his gaunt, quivering body, Silver-Leg laughed with gentle irony, as a man would laugh at the impotent vapourings of a child.

"Or what, my good Hare-Lip?" he queried slowly.

Then as the other instinctively lowered his gaze and mumbled something between his teeth, Silver-Leg shrugged his shoulders and said with kind indulgence, still as if he were speaking to a child:

"Madame will settle, my friend. Do not worry. It is bad to worry. You remember Fear-Nought: he took to worrying--just as you are doing now--wanted to be paid out of his turn, or more than his share, I forget which. But you remember him?"

"I do," muttered Hare-Lip with a savage oath. "Fear-Nought was tracked down by the police and dragged to Vincennes, or Force, or Bicêtre--we never knew."

"To the guillotine, my good Hare-Lip," rejoined Silver-Leg blandly, "along with some other very brave Chouans like yourselves, who also had given their leaders some considerable trouble."

"Betrayed by you," growled Hare-Lip menacingly.

"Punished--that's all," concluded Silver-Leg as he once more turned to go.

"Treachery is a game at which more than one can play."

"The stakes are high. And only one man can win," remarked Silver-Leg dryly.

"And one man must lose," shouted Hare-Lip, now beside himself with rage, "and that one shall be you this time, my fine Silver-Leg. À moi, my mates!" he called to his companions.

And in a moment the men fell on Silver-Leg with the vigour born of terror and greed, and for the first moment or two of their desperate tussle it seemed as if the man with the wooden leg must succumb to the fury of his assailants. Darkness encompassed them all round, and the deep silence which dwells in the heart of the woods. And in the darkness and the silence these men fought--and fought desperately--for the possession of a few hundred francs just filched at the muzzle of a pistol from a few peaceable travellers.

Pistols of course could not be used; the police patrols might not be far away, and so they fought on in silence, grim and determined, one man against half a dozen, and that one halt, and weighted with the spoils. But he had the strength of a giant, and with his back against a stately fir tree he used the heavy wallet as a flail, keeping his assailants at arm's length with the menace of death-dealing blows.

Then, suddenly, from far away, even through the dull thuds of this weird and grim struggle, there came the sound of men approaching--the click of sabres, the tramp and snorting of horses, the sense of men moving rapidly even if cautiously through the gloom. Silver-Leg was the first to hear it.

"Hush!" he cried suddenly, and as loudly as he dared, "the police!"

Again, with that blind instinct born of terror and ever-present danger, the others obeyed. The common peril had as swiftly extinguished the quarrel as greed of gain had fanned it into flame.

The cavalcade was manifestly drawing nearer.

"Disperse!" commanded Silver-Leg under his breath. "Clear out of the wood, but avoid the tracks which lead out of it, lest it is surrounded. Remember 'Corinne' for Monseigneur, and that Red-Poll can have the key for Madame on Friday."

Once again he had made use of his opportunity. Before the others had recovered from, their sudden fright, he had quietly stumped away, and in less than five seconds was lost in the gloom among the trees. For a moment or two longer an ear, attuned by terror or the constant sense of danger, might have perceived the dull, uneven thud of his wooden leg against the soft carpet of pine needles, but even this soon died away in the distance, and over the kingdom of darkness which held sway within the forest there fell once more the pall of deathlike silence. The posse of police in search of human quarry had come and gone, the stealthy footsteps of tracked criminals had ceased to resound from tree to tree; all that could be heard was the occasional call of a night-bird, or the furtive movement of tiny creatures of the wild.

Silence hung over the forest for close upon an hour. Then from behind a noble fir a dark figure detached itself and more stealthily, more furtively than any tiny beast it stole along the track which leads to the main road. The figure, wrapped in a dark mantle, glided determinedly along despite the difficulties of the narrow track, complicated now by absolute darkness. Hours went by ere it reached the main road, on the very spot where some few hours ago the mail-coach had been held up and robbed by a pack of impudent thieves. Here the figure halted for awhile, and just then the heavy rain clouds, which had hung over the sky the whole evening, slowly parted and revealed the pale waning moon. A soft light gradually suffused the sky and vanquished the impenetrable darkness.

Not a living soul was in sight save that solitary figure by the roadside--a man, to all appearances, wearing a broad-brimmed hat casting a deep shadow over his face; the waning moon threw a cold light upon the grey mantle which he wore. On ahead the exquisite tower of the church of Notre Dame appeared vague and fairylike against the deep sapphire of the horizon far away. Then the solitary figure started to walk briskly in the direction of the city.

III

M. le Procureur Impérial, sitting in his comfortable armchair in the well-furnished apartment which he occupied in the Rue St. Blaise at Alençon, was surveying his visitor with a quizzical and questioning gaze.

On the desk before him lay the letter which that same visitor had presented to him the previous evening--a letter penned by no less a hand than that of M. le Duc d'Otrante himself, Minister of Police, and recommending the bearer of this august autograph to the good will of M. de Saint-Tropèze, Procureur Impérial at the tribunal of Alençon. Nay, more! M. le Ministre in that same autograph letter gave orders, in no grudging terms, that the bearer was to be trusted implicitly, and that every facility was to be given him in the execution of his duty: said duty consisting in the tracking down and helping to bring to justice of as many as possible of those saucy Chouans who, not content with terrorising the countryside, were up in arms against the government of His Imperial Majesty.

A direct encroachment this on the rights and duties of M. le Procureur Impérial; no wonder he surveyed the quiet, insignificant-looking individual before him, with a not altogether benevolent air.

M. le préfet sitting on the opposite side of the high mantelpiece was discreetly silent until his chief chose to speak.

After a brief while the Procureur Impérial addressed his visitor.

"Monsieur le Duc d'Otrante," he said in that dry, supercilious tone which he was wont to affect when addressing his subordinates, "speaks very highly of you, Monsieur--Monsieur--By the way, the Minister, I perceive, does not mention your name. What is your name, Monsieur?"

"Fernand, Monsieur le Procureur," replied the man.

"Fernand? Fernand what?"

"Nothing, Monsieur le Procureur. Only Fernand."

The little Man in Grey spoke very quietly in a dull, colourless tone which harmonised with the neutral tone of his whole appearance. For a moment it seemed as if a peremptory or sarcastic retort hovered on M. le Procureurs lips. The man's quietude appeared like an impertinence. M. de Saint-Tropèze belonged to the old Noblesse. He had emigrated at the time of the Revolution and spent a certain number of years in England, during which time a faithful and obscure steward administered his property and saved it from confiscation.

The blandishments of the newly-crowned Emperor had lured M. de Saint-Tropèze back to France. Common sense and ambition had seemingly got the better of his antiquated ideals, whilst Napoleon was only too ready to surround himself with as many scions of the ancient nobility as were willing to swear allegiance to him. He welcomed Henri de Saint-Tropèze and showered dignities upon him with a lavish hand; but the latter never forgot that the Government he now served was an upstart one, and he never departed from that air of condescension and high breeding which kept him aloof from his more plebeian subordinates and which gave him an authority and an influence in the province which they themselves could never hope to attain.

M. le préfet had coughed discreetly. The warning was well-timed. He knew every word of the Minister's letter by heart, and one phrase in it might, he feared, have escaped M. le Procureur's notice. It ordered that the bearer of the Ministerial credentials was to be taken entirely on trust--no questions were to be asked of him save those to which he desired to make reply. To disregard even the vaguest hint given by the all-powerful Minister of Police was, to say the least, hazardous. Fortunately M. de Saint-Tropèze understood the warning. He pressed his thin lips tightly together and did not pursue the subject of his visitor's name any farther.

"You propose setting to work immediately, Monsieur--er--Fernand?" he asked with frigid hauteur.

"With your permission, Monsieur le Procureur," replied the Man in Grey.

"In the matter of the highway robbery the other night, for instance?"

"In that and other matters, Monsieur le Procureur."

"You were on the coach which was attacked by those damnable Chouans, I believe?"

"Yes, Monsieur le Procureur. I picked up the coach at Argentan and sat next to the driver until the vehicle was ordered to halt."

"Then what happened?"

"A man scrambled up on the box-seat beside me, and holding a pistol to my head commanded me to descend."

"And you descended?"

"Yes," replied the man quietly. He paused a moment and then added by way of an explanation: "I hurt my knee coming down; the pain caused me to lose some measure of consciousness. When I returned to my senses, I found myself on the roadside--all alone--there was no sign either of the coach or of the footpads."

"An unfortunate beginning," said M. de Saint-Tropèze with a distinct note of sarcasm in his voice, "for a secret agent of His Majesty's Police sent down to track some of the most astute rascals known in the history of crime."

"I hope to do better in the future, Monsieur le Procureur," rejoined the Man in Grey simply.

M. de Saint-Tropèze made no further remark, and for a moment or two there was silence in the room. The massive Louis XIV clock ticked monotonously; M. de Saint-Tropèze seemed to be dissociating his well-bred person from the sordid and tortuous affairs of the Police. The Man in Grey appeared to be waiting until he was spoken to again, and M. le préfet had a vague feeling that the silence was becoming oppressive, as if some unspoken enmity lurked between the plebeian and obscure police agent and the highly connected and influential Procurator of His Majesty the Emperor. He threw himself blandly into the breach.

"Of course, of course," he said genially. "You, Monsieur--er--Fernand, are lucky to have escaped with your life. Those rascals stick at nothing nowadays. The driver of the coach fully believed that you had been murdered. I suppose you saw nothing of the rogue?"

But this was evidently not one of the questions which the Man in Grey had any desire to answer, and M. Vimars did not insist. He turned obsequiously to M. le Procureur.

"The driver," he said, "spoke of one having a wooden leg. But the worthy Gontran was very vague in all his statements. I imagine that he and all the male passengers must have behaved like cowards or the rascals would never have got so clean away."

"The night was very dark, Monsieur le Préfet," observed the Man in Grey dryly, "and the Chouans were well armed."

"Quite so," here broke in M. le Procureur impatiently, "and no object can be served now in recriminations. See to it, my good Vimars," he continued in a tone that was still slightly sarcastic but entirely peremptory, "that the Minister's orders are obeyed to the last letter. Place yourself and all your personnel and the whole of the local police at Monsieur--er--Fernand's disposal, and do not let me hear any more complaints of inefficiency or want of good will on your part until those scoundrels have been laid by the heel."

IV

M. de Saint-Tropèze paused after his peroration. With an almost imperceptible nod of his handsome head he indicated both to his visitor and to his subordinate that the audience was at an end. But M. le préfet, though he knew himself to be dismissed, appeared reluctant to go. There was something which M. le Procureur had forgotten, and the worthy préfet was trying to gather up courage to jog his memory. He had a mightily wholesome respect for his chief, had M. Vimars, for the Procureur was not only a man of vast erudition and of the bluest blood, but one who was held in high consideration by His Majesty's government in Paris, ay, and, so 'twas said, by His Majesty himself.

So M. Vimars hummed and hawed and gave one or two discreet little coughs, whilst M. le Procureur with obvious impatience was drumming his well-manicured nails against the arm of his chair. At last he said testily:

"You have something you wish to say to me, my good Monsieur Vimars?"

"Yes, Monsieur le Procureur," hazarded the préfet in reply, "that is--there is the matter of the burglary--and--and the murder last night--that is----"

M. le Procureur frowned: "Those are local matters," he said loftily, "which concern the commissary of police, my good Vimars, and are beneath the notice of Monsieur le Ministre's secret agent."

The préfet, conscious of a reprimand, blushed to the very roots of his scanty hair. He rose with some haste and the obvious desire to conceal his discomfiture in a precipitate retreat, when the Man in Grey interposed in his quiet, even monotone:

"Nothing is beneath the notice of a secret agent, Monsieur le Procureur," he said; "and everything which is within the province of the commissary of police concerns the representative of the Minister."

M. Vimars literally gasped at this presumption. How anyone dared thus to run counter to M. le Procureur's orders simply passed his comprehension. He looked with positive horror on the meagre, insignificant personage who even now was meeting M. le Procureur's haughty, supercilious glance without any sign of contrition or of shame.

M. de Saint-Tropèze had raised his aristocratic eyebrows, and tried to wither the audacious malapert with his scornful glance, but the little Man in Grey appeared quite unconscious of the enormity of his offence; he stood by--as was his wont--quietly and silently, his eyes fixed inquiringly on the préfet, who was indeed hoping that the floor would open conveniently and swallow him up ere he was called upon to decide whether he should obey the orders of his official chief, or pay heed to the commands of the accredited agent of M. the Minister of Police.

But M. le Procureur decided the question himself and in the only way possible. The Minister's letter with its peremptory commands lay there before him--the secret agent of His Majesty's Police was to be aided and obeyed implicitly in all matters relating to his work; there was nothing to be done save to comply with those orders as graciously as he could, and without further loss of dignity.

"You have heard the wishes of Monsieur le Ministre's agent, my good Vimars," he said coldly; "so I pray you speak to him of the matter which exercises your mind, for of a truth I am not well acquainted with all the details!"

Whereupon he fell to contemplating the exquisite polish on his almond-shaped nails. Though the overbearing little upstart in the grey coat could command the obsequiousness of such men as that fool Vimars, he must be shown at the outset that his insolence would find no weak spot in the armour of M. de Saint-Tropèze's lofty self-respect.

"Oh! it is very obvious," quoth the préfet, whose only desire was to conciliate both parties, "that the matter is not one which affects the graver question of those satané Chouans. At the same time both the affairs of last night are certainly mysterious and present some unusual features which have greatly puzzled our exceedingly able commissary of police. It seems that in the early hours of this morning the library of Monseigneur the Constitutional Bishop of Alençon was broken into by thieves. Fortunately nothing of any value was stolen, and this part of the affair appeared simple enough, until an hour or two later a couple of peasants, who were walking from Lonrai towards the city, came across the body of a man lying face upwards by the roadside. The man was quite dead--had been dead some time apparently. The two louts hurried at once to the commissariat of police and made their depositions. Monsieur Lefèvre, our chief commissary, proceeded to the scene of the crime; he has now the affair in hand."

The préfet had perforce to pause in his narrative for lack of breath. He had been talking volubly and uninterruptedly, and indeed he had no cause to complain of lack of attention on the part of his hearer. M. le Ministre's secret agent sat absolutely still, his deep-set eyes fixed intently upon the narrator. Alone M. le Procureur Impérial maintained his attitude of calm disdain. He still appeared deeply absorbed in the contemplation of his finger-nails.

"At first," resumed the préfet after his dramatic pause, "these two crimes, the greater and the less, seemed in no way connected, and personally I am not sure even now that they are. A certain air of similarity and mystery, however, clings to them both, for in both cases the crimes appear at the outset so very purposeless. In the case of the burglary in Monseigneur's palace the thieves were obviously scared before they could lay hands on any valuables, but even so there were some small pieces of silver lying about which they might have snatched up, even if they were in a vast hurry to get away; whilst in the case of the murder, though the victim's silver watch was stolen and his pockets ransacked, the man was obviously poor and not worth knocking down."

"And is the identity of the victim known to the police?" here asked the Man in Grey in his dull, colourless voice.

"Indeed it is," replied the préfet; "the man was well known throughout the neighbourhood. He was valet to Madame la Marquise de Phélan."

M. le Procureur looked up suddenly from his engrossing occupation.

"Ah!" he said, "I did not know that. Lefèvre did not tell me that he had established the identity of the victim."

He sighed and once more gazed meditatively upon his finger-nails.

"Poor Maxence! I have often seen him at Plélan. There never was a more inoffensive creature. What motive could the brute have for such a villainous murder?"

The préfet shrugged his shoulders.

"Some private quarrel, I imagine," he said.

"A love affair?" queried the Man in Grey.

"Oh no, Monsieur. Maxence was the wrong side of fifty."

"A smart man?"

"Anything but smart--a curious, shock-headed, slouchy-looking person with hair as red as a fox's."

Just for the space of one second the colourless eyes of the Man in Grey lit up with a quick and intense light; it seemed for the moment as if an exclamation difficult to suppress would escape his thin, bloodless lips, and his whole insignificant figure appeared to be quivering with a sudden, uncontrollable eagerness. But this departure from his usual quietude was so momentary that M. le préfet failed to notice it, whilst M. le Procureur remained as usual uninterested and detached.

"Poor Maxence!" resumed M. Vimars after awhile. "He had, as far as is known, not a single enemy in the world. He was devoted to Madame la Marquise and enjoyed her complete confidence; he was not possessed of any savings, nor was he of a quarrelsome disposition. He can't have had more than a few francs about his person when he was so foully waylaid and murdered. Indeed, it is because the crime is ostensibly so wanton that the police at once dismissed the idea that those abominable Chouans had anything to do with it!"

"Is the road where the body was found very lonely of nights?" asked the Man in Grey.

"It is a lonely road," replied the préfet, "and never considered very safe, as it is a favourite haunt of the Chouans--but it is the direct road between Alençon and Mayenne, through Lonrai and Plélan."

"Is it known what business took the confidential valet of Madame la Marquise de Plélan on that lonely road in the middle of the night?"

"It has not been definitely established," here broke in M. le Procureur curtly, "that the murder was committed in the middle of the night."

"I thought----"

"The body was found in the early morning," continued M. de Saint-Tropèze with an air of cold condescension; "the man had been dead some hours--the leech has not pronounced how many. Maxence had no doubt many friends or relations in Alençon: it is presumed that he spent the afternoon in the city and was on his way back to Plélan in the evening when he was waylaid and murdered."

"That presumption is wrong," said the Man in Grey quietly.

"Wrong?" retorted M. le Procureur frigidly.

"What do you mean?"

"I was walking home from Plélan towards Alençon in the small hours of the morning. There was no dead body lying in the road then."

"The body lay by the roadside, half in the ditch," said M. le Procureur dryly, "you may have missed seeing it."

"Possibly," rejoined the Man in Grey equally dryly, "but unlikely."

"Were you looking out for it then?" riposted the Procureur. But no sooner were the words out of his mouth than he realised his mistake. The Man in Grey made no reply; he literally appeared to withdraw himself into an invisible shell, to efface himself yet further within a colourless atmosphere, out of which it was obviously unwise to try to drag him.

M. le Procureur pressed his thin lips together, impatient with himself at an unnecessary loss of dignity. As usual M. le préfet was ready to throw himself into the breach.

"I am sure," he said with his usual volubility, "that we are wasting Monsieur le Procureur's valuable time now. I can assure you, Monsieur--er--Fernand, that our chief commissary of police can give you all the details of the crime--if, indeed, they interest you. Shall we go now?--that is," he added, with that same feeling of hesitation which overcame him every time he encountered the secret agent's calm, inquiring look, "that is--er--unless there's anything else you wish to ask of Monsieur le Procureur."

"I wish to know with regard to the murder, what was the cause of death," said the Man in Grey quietly.

"A pistol shot, sir," replied M. de Saint-Tropèze coldly, "right between the shoulder blades, delivered at short range apparently, seeing that the man's coat was charred and blackened with powder. The leech avers that he must have fallen instantly."

"Shot between the shoulders, and yet found lying on his back," murmured the Man in Grey. "And was nothing at all found upon the body that would give a clue to the motive of the crime?"

"Nothing, my dear sir," broke in the préfet glibly, "nothing at all. In his breeches' pocket there was a greasy and crumpled sheet of letter-paper, which on examination was found to be covered with a row of numerals all at random--like a child's exercise-book."

"Could I see the paper?"

"It is at the commissariat of police," explained the Procureur curtly.

"Where I can easily find it, of course," concluded the Man in Grey with calm decision. "In the meanwhile perhaps Monsieur le préfet will be kind enough to tell me something more about the burglary at the Archbishop's Palace."

"There's very little to tell, my good Monsieur Fernand," said M. Vimars, who, far more conscious than was the stranger of the Procureur's growing impatience, would have given a month's salary for the privilege of making himself scarce.

"With what booty did the burglars make off?"

"With nothing of any value; and what they did get they dropped in their flight. The police found a small silver candlestick, and a brass paper weight in the street close to the gate of Monseigneur's Palace, also one or two books which no doubt the burglars had seized in the hope that they were valuable editions."

"Nothing, then, has actually been stolen?"

"Nothing. I believe that Monseigneur told the chief commissary that one or two of his books are still missing, but none of any value. So you see, my good Monsieur--er--Fernand," concluded M. Vimars blandly, "that the whole matter is quite beneath your consideration. It is a case of a vulgar murder with only a private grudge by way of motive--and an equally vulgar attempt at burglary, fortunately with no evil results. Our local police--though none too efficient, alas! in these strenuous days, when His Majesty's army claims the flower of our manhood--is well able to cope with these simple matters, which, of course, must occur in every district from time to time. You may take it from me--and I have plenty of experience, remember--that the matter has no concern whatever with the Chouans and with your mission here. You can, quite conscientiously, devote the whole of your time to the case of the highway robbery the other night, and the recovery of the sixty-two hundred francs which were stolen from the coach, as well as the tracking of that daring rascal with the wooden leg."

Satisfied with his peroration, M. Vimars at last felt justified in moving towards the door.

"I don't think," he concluded with suave obsequiousness, "that we need take up any more of Monsieur le Procureur's valuable time, and with his gracious permission----"

To his intense relief, M. Vimars perceived that the Man in Grey was at last prepared to take his leave.

M. de Saint-Tropèze, plainly at the end of his patience, delighted to be rid of his tiresome visitors, at once became pleasantly condescending. To the secret agent of His Majesty's Police he gave a quite gracious nod, and made the worthy préfet proud and happy by whispering in his ear:

"Do not allow that little busybody to interfere with you too much, my dear Monsieur Vimars. I am prepared to back your skill and experience in such matters against any young shrimp from Paris."

The nod of understanding which accompanied this affable speech sent M. Vimars into an empyrean of delight. After which M. le Procureur finally bowed his visitors out of the room.

The little Man in Grey walked in silence beside M. Vimars along the narrow network of streets which lead to the Hôtel de Ville. The préfet had a suite of apartments assigned to him in the building, and once he was installed in his own well-furnished library, untrammelled by the presence of his chief, and with the accredited agent of His Majesty's Minister sitting opposite to him, he gave full rein to his own desire for perfect amity with so important a personage.

He began by a lengthy disquisition on the merits of M. le Procureur Impérial. Never had there been a man of such consideration and of such high culture in the city. M. de Saint-Tropèze was respected alike by the municipal officials, by the townspeople and by the landed aristocracy of the neighbourhood--and he was a veritable terror to the light-fingered gentry, as well as to the gangs of Chouans that infested the district.

The Man in Grey listened to the fulsome panegyric with his accustomed deep attention. He asked a few questions as to M. de Saint-Tropèze's domestic circumstances. "Was he married?" "Was he wealthy?" "Did he keep up a luxurious mode of life?"

To all these questions M. Vimars was only too ready to give reply. No, Monsieur le Procureur was not married. He was presumably wealthy, for he kept up a very elegant bachelor establishment in the Rue St. Blaise with just a few old and confidential servants. The sources of his income were not known, as Monsieur de Saint-Tropèze was very proud and reserved, and would not condescend to speak of his affairs with anyone.

Next the worthy préfet harked back, with wonted volubility, to the double outrage of the previous night, and rehearsed at copious length every circumstance connected with it. Strangely enough, the secret agent who had been sent by the Minister all the way from Paris in order to track down that particular band of Chouans, appeared far more interested in the murder of Mme. de Plélan's valet and the theft of a few books out of Monseigneur the Bishop's library than he was in the daring robbery of the mail-coach.

"You knew the unfortunate Maxence, did you not, Monsieur le Préfet?" he asked.

"Why, yes," replied M. Vimars, "for I have often paid my respects to Madame la Marquise de Plélan."

"What was he like?"

"You can go over to the commissariat of police and see what's left of the poor man," rejoined the préfet, with a feeble attempt at grim humour. "The most remarkable feature about him was his red hair--an unusual colour among our Normandy peasantry."

Later M. Vimars put the finishing touch to his amiability by placing his services unreservedly at the disposal of M. le Ministre's agent.

"Is there anything that I can do for you, my good Monsieur Fernand?" he asked urbanely.

"Not for the moment, I thank you," replied Fernand. "I will send to you if I require any assistance from the police. But in the meanwhile," he added, "I see that you are something of a scholar. I should be greatly obliged if you could lend me a book to while away some of my idle hours."

"A book? With pleasure!" quoth M. Vimars, not a little puzzled. "But how did you know?"

"That you were a scholar?" rejoined the other with a vague smile. "It was a fairly simple guess, seeing your well-stocked cases of books around me, and that a well-fingered volume protrudes even now from your coat-pocket."

"Ah! Ah!" retorted the préfet ingenuously, "I see that truly you are a great deal sharper, Monsieur Fernand, than you appear to be. But in any case," he added, "I shall be charmed to be of service to you in the matter of my small library. I flatter myself that it is both comprehensive and select--so if there is anything you especially desire to read----"

"I thank you, Sir," said the Man in Grey; "as a matter of fact I have never had the opportunity of reading Madame de Staël's latest work, Corinne, and if you happen to possess a copy----"

"With the greatest of pleasure, my dear sir," exclaimed the préfet. He went at once to one of his well-filled bookcases, and after a brief search found the volume and handed it with a smile to his visitor.

"It seems a grave pity," he added, "that no new edition of this remarkable work has ever been printed. But Madame de Staël is not in favour with His Majesty, which no doubt accounts for the publisher's lack of enterprise."

A few more words of polite farewell: after which M. Vimars took final leave of the Minister's agent.

The little Man in Grey glided out of the stately apartment like a ghost, even his footsteps failing to resound along the polished floor.

V

Buried in a capacious armchair, beside a cheerfully blazing fire, M. le Procureur Impérial had allowed the copy of the Moniteur which he had been reading to drop from his shapely hands on to the floor. He had closed his eyes and half an hour had gone by in peaceful somnolence, even while M. Lefèvre, chief commissary of police, was cooling his heels in the antechamber, preparatory to being received in audience on most urgent business.

M. le Procureur Impérial never did anything in a hurry, and, on principle, always kept a subordinate waiting until any officiousness or impertinence which might have been lurking in the latter's mind had been duly squelched by weariness and sore feet.

So it was only after he had indulged in a short and refreshing nap that M. de Saint-Tropèze rang for his servant, and ordered him to introduce M. Lefèvre, chief commissary of police. The latter, a choleric, apoplectic, loud-voiced official, entered the audience chamber in a distinctly chastened spirit. He had been shown the original letter of credentials sent to M. le Procureur by the Minister, and yesterday he had caught sight of the small grey-clad figure as it flitted noiselessly along the narrow streets of the city. And inwardly the brave commissary of police had then and there perpetrated an act of high treason, for he had sworn at the ineptitude of the grand Ministries in Paris, which sent a pack of incompetent agents to interfere with those who were capable of dealing with their own local affairs.

Monsieur le Procureur Impérial, who no doubt sympathised with the worthy man's grievances, was inclined to be gracious.

"Well? And what is it now, my good Monsieur Lefèvre?" he asked as soon as the commissary was seated.

"In one moment, Monsieur le Procureur," growled Lefèvre. "First of all, will you tell me what I am to do about that secret agent who has come here, I suppose, to poke his ugly nose into my affairs?"

"What you are to do about him?" rejoined M. de Saint-Tropèze with a smile. "I have shown you the Minister's letter: he says that we must leave all matters in the hands of his accredited agent."

"By your leave," quoth Lefèvre wrathfully, "that accredited agent might as well be polishing the flagstones of the Paris boulevards, for all the good that he will do down here."

"You think so?" queried M. le Procureur, and with a detached air, he fell into his customary contemplation of his nails. "And with your permission," continued the commissary, "I will proceed with my own investigations of the outrages committed by those abominable Chouans, for that bundle of conceit will never get the hang of the affair."

"But the Minister says that we must not interfere. We must render all the assistance that we can."

"Bah! we'll render assistance when it is needed," retorted Lefèvre captiously. "But in the meantime I am not going to let that wooden-legged scoundrel slip through my fingers, to please any grey-coated marmoset who thinks he can lord it over me in my own district."

M. de Saint-Tropèze appeared interested.

"You have a clue?" he asked.

"More than that. I know who killed Maxence."

"Ah! You have got the man? Well done, my brave Lefèvre," exclaimed M. le Procureur, without, however, a very great show of enthusiasm.

"I haven't got him yet," parried Lefèvre. "But I have the description of the rascal. A little patience and I can lay my hands on him--provided that busybody does not interfere."

"Who is he, then?" queried M. de Saint-Tropèze.

"One of those damned Chouans."

"You are sure?"

"Absolutely. All day yesterday I was busy interrogating witnesses, who I knew must have been along the road between Lonrai and the city in the small hours of the morning--workpeople and so on, who go to and from their work every morning of their lives. Well! after a good deal of trouble we have been able to establish that the murder was actually committed between the hours of five and half-past, because although no one appears actually to have heard the pistol shot, the people who were on the road before five saw nothing suspicious, whilst the two louts who subsequently discovered the body actually heard the tower clock of Notre Dame striking the half-hour at the very time."

"Well? And----"

"No fewer than three of the witnesses state that they saw a man with a queer-shaped lip, dressed in a ragged coat and breeches, and with stockingless feet thrust into sabots, hanging about the road shortly before five o'clock. They gave him a wide berth, for they took him to be a Chouan on the prowl."

"Why should a Chouan trouble to kill a wretched man who has not a five-franc piece to bless himself with?"

"That's what we've got to find out," rejoined the commissary of police, "and we will find it out, too, as soon as we've got the ruffian and the rest of the gang. I know the rogue, mind you--the man with the queer lip. I have had my eye on him for some time. Oh! he belongs to the gang, I'll stake mine oath on it: a youngish man who should be in the army and is obviously a deserter--a ne'er-do-well who never does a day's honest work and disappears o' nights. What his name is and where he comes from I do not know. But through him we'll get the others, including the chief of the gang--the man with the wooden leg."

"God grant you may succeed!" ejaculated M. le Procureur sententiously. "These perpetual outrages in one's district are a fearful strain on one's nerves. By the way," he added, as he passed his shapely hand over a number of miscellaneous papers which lay in a heap upon his desk, "I don't usually take heed of anonymous letters, but one came to me this morning which might be worth your consideration."

He selected a tattered, greasy paper from the heap, fingering it gingerly, and having carefully unfolded it passed it across the table to the chief commissary of police. Lefèvre smoothed the paper out: the writing was almost illegible, and grease and dirt had helped further to confuse the characters, but the commissary had had some experience of such communications, and contrived slowly to decipher the scrawl.

"It is a denunciation, of course," he said. "The rogues appear to be quarrelling amongst themselves. 'If,' says the writer of the epistle, 'M. le Procureur will send his police to-night between the hours of ten and twelve to the Cache-Renard woods and they follow the directions given below, they will come across the money and valuables which were taken from the mail-coach last Wednesday, and also those who robbed the coach and murdered Mme. de Pléllan's valet. Strike the first bridle-path on the right after entering the wood by the main road, until you come to a fallen fir tree lying across another narrow path; dismount here and follow this track for a further three hundred mètres, till you come to a group of five larches in the midst of a thicket of birch and oak. Stand with your back to the larch that is farthest from you, and face the thicket; there you will perceive another track which runs straight into the depths of the wood, follow it until you come to a tiny clearing, at the bottom of which the thicket will seem so dense that you would deem it impenetrable. Plunge into it boldly to where a nest of broken branches reveals the presence of human footsteps, and in front of you you will see a kind of hut composed of dead branches and caked mud and covered with a rough thatch of heather. In that hut you will find that for which you seek.'"

"Do you think it worth while to act upon this anonymous denunciation?" queried M. Saint-Tropèze when Lefèvre had finished reading.

"I certainly do," replied the commissary. "In any case it can do no harm."

"You must take plenty of men with you."

"Leave that to me, Monsieur le Procureur," rejoined Lefèvre, "and I'll see that they are well armed, too."

"What about the secret agent?"

Lefèvre swore.

"That worm?" was his sole but very expressive comment.

"Will you see him about the matter?"

"What do you think?"

"I suppose you must."

"And if he gives me orders?"

"You must obey them, of course. Have you seen him this morning?"

"Yes. He had ordered me to come to his lodgings in the Rue de France."

"What did he want?"

"The scrap of paper which we had found in the breeches' pocket of Maxence."

"You gave it to him?"

"Of course," growled Lefèvre savagely. "Haven't we all got to obey him?"

"You left him in his lodgings, then?"

"Yes."

"Doing what?"

"Reading a book."

"Reading a book?" exclaimed M. de Saint-Tropèze with a harsh laugh. "What book?"

"I just noticed the title," replied Lefèvre, "though I'm nothing of a scholar and books don't interest me."

"What was the title?"

"Corinne," said the commissary of police.

Apparently M. le Procureur Impérial had come to the end of the questions which he desired to put to the worthy M. Lefèvre, for he said nothing more, but remained leaning back in his chair and gazing straight out of the window beside him. His pale, aristocratic profile looked almost like chiselled marble against the purple damask of the cushions. He seemed absorbed in thought, or else supremely bored; M. Lefèvre--nothing of a psychologist, despite his calling--could not have said which.

The ticking of the massive Louis XIV clock upon the mantelpiece and the sizzling of damp wood on the hearth alone broke the silence which reigned in the stately apartment. Through the closed window the manifold sounds which emanate from a busy city came discreet and subdued.

Instinctively M. Lefèvre's glance followed that of his chief: he, too, fell to gazing out of the window where only a few passers-by were seen hurrying homewards on this late dreary October afternoon. Suddenly he perceived the narrow, shrinking figure of the little Man in Grey gliding swiftly down the narrow street. The commissary of police smothered the savage oath which had risen to his lips: he turned to his chief, and even his obtuse perceptions were aroused by what he saw. M. le Procureur Impérial was no longer leaning back listlessly against the damask cushions: he was leaning forward, his fine, white hands clutching the arms of his chair. He, too, had apparently caught sight of the grey-clad figure, for his eyes, wide open and resentful, followed it as it glided along, and on his whole face there was such an expression of hatred and savagery that the worthy commissary felt unaccountably awed and subdued. Next moment, however, he thought he must have been dreaming, for M. de Saint-Tropèze had once more turned to him with that frigid urbanity which became his aristocratic personality so well.

"Well, my good Lefèvre," he said, "I don't really think that I can help you further in any way. I quite appreciate your mistrust of the obtrusive stranger, and personally I cannot avoid a suspicion that he will hamper you by interfering at a critical moment to-night during your expedition against the Chouans. He may just be the cause of their slipping through your fingers, which would be such a terrible pity now that you have gathered the net so skilfully around them."

Lefèvre rose, and with firm, deliberate movements tightened the belt around his portly waist, re-adjusted the set of his tunic, and generally contrived to give himself an air of determination and energy.

"I'll say nothing to the shrimp about our expedition to-night," he said with sullen resolution. "That is, unless you, Monsieur le Procureur, give me orders to do so."

"Oh, I?" rejoined M. de Saint-Tropèze carelessly. "I won't say anything one way or the other. The whole matter is out of my hands and you must act as you think best. Whatever happens," he added slowly and emphatically, "you will get no blame from me."

Which was such an extraordinary thing for M. le Procureur to say--who was one of the most pedantic, censorious and autocratic of men--that the good Lefèvre spoke of it afterwards to M. le préfet and to one or two of his friends. He could not understand this attitude of humility and obedience on the part of his chief: but everyone agreed that it was small wonder M. le Procureur Impérial was upset, seeing that the presence of that secret police agent in Alençon was a direct snub to all the municipal and departmental authorities throughout the district, and M. de Saint-Tropèze was sure to resent it more than anyone else, for he was very proud, and acknowledged to be one of the most capable of highly-placed officials in the whole of France.

VI

The night that followed was unusually dark. Out in the Cache-Renard woods the patter of the rain on the tall crests of the pines and the soughing of the wind through the branches of the trees drowned every other sound. In the burrow built of dead branches, caked mud and dried heather, five men sat waiting, their ears strained to the crackling of every tiny twig, to the fall of every drop of moisture from the over-laden twigs. Among them the dark lantern threw a dim, flickering light on their sullen, glowering faces. Despite the cold and the damp outside, the atmosphere within was hot to suffocation; the men's breath came panting and laboured, and now and again they exchanged a few whispered words.

"In any case," declared one of them, "if we feel that he is playing us false we shall have to do for him to-night, eh, mates?"

A kind of muffled assent went round the circle, and one man murmured:

"Do you really mistrust him, Hare-Lip?"

"I should," replied Hare-Lip curtly, "if I thought, he knew about Red-Poll."

"You don't think that he suspects?" queried another.

"I don't see how he can. He can't have shown his face, or rather his wooden leg inside Alençon since the mail-coach episode. The police are keen after him. But if he did hear rumours of the death of Red-Poll he will also have heard that the murder was only an ordinary case of robbery--watch and money stolen--and that a sheet of letter-paper covered with random numerals was found in the breeches' pocket of the murdered man."

One of the men swore lustily in the dark.

"The paper covered with numerals!" he muttered savagely under his breath. "You clumsy fool to have left that behind!"

"What was the use----" began another.

But Hare-Lip laughed, and broke in quietly:

"Do ye take me for a fool, mates? I was not going to take away that original sheet of paper and proclaim it to our chiefs that it was one of us who killed Red-Poll. No! I took the sheet of letter-paper with me when I went to meet Red-Poll. After he fell--I shot him between the shoulders--I turned him over on his back and ransacked his pockets; that was a blind. Then I found the paper with the figures and copied them out carefully--that was another blind,--in case Silver-Leg heard of the affair and suspected us."

One or two of the others gave a growl of dissent.

"You might have been caught while you were playing that silly game," said one of the men, "which would not deceive a child."

"Silver-Leg is no gaby," murmured another.

"Well, he'll be here anon," concluded Hare-Lip lightly. "If you think he means to play a dirty trick, he can go and join Red-Poll, that's all."

"He may not come, after all."

"He must come. I had his message to meet him here to-night without fail. The chiefs have planned another attack: on the Orleans coach this time. Silver-Leg wants us to be of the party."

"We ought to have got hold of the last booty before now!"

"Impossible! Mole-Skin and I have not figured out all the directions from the book and the numerals yet. It is not an easy task, I tell you, but it shall be done soon, and we can take you straight to the spot as soon as we have the directions before us."

"Unless Silver-Leg and Madame remove the booty in the meanwhile," grunted one of the party caustically.

"I sometimes wonder----" said another. But he got no further. A peremptory "Hush!" from Hare-Lip suddenly silenced them all.

With a swift movement one of them extinguished the lanthorn, and now they cowered in absolute darkness within their burrow like so many wild beasts tracked to earth by the hunters. The heat was suffocating: the men vainly tried to subdue the sound of their breath as it came panting from their parched throats.

"The police!" Hare-Lip muttered hoarsely.

But they did not need to he told. Just like tracked beasts they knew every sound which portended danger, and already from afar off, even from the very edge of the wood, more than a kilométre away, their cars, attuned to every sound, had perceived the measured tramp of horses upon the soft, muddy road. They cowered there, rigid and silent. The darkness encompassed them, and they felt safe enough in their shelter in the very heart of the woods, in this secret hiding-place which was known to no living soul save to them. The police on patrol duty had often passed them by: the nearest track practicable on horseback was four hundred mètres, away, the nearest footpath made a wide détour round the thicket, wherein these skulking miscreants had contrived to build their lair.

As a rule, it meant cowering, silent and motionless, inside the burrow whilst perhaps one posse of police, more venturesome than most, had dismounted at the end of the bridle-path and plunged afoot into the narrower track, scouring the thicket on either side for human quarry. It involved only an elementary amount of danger, distant and intangible, not worth an accelerated heart-beat, or even a gripping of knife or pistol wherewith to sell life and liberty at a price.

And so, for the first five minutes, while the tramp of horses' hoofs drew nearer, the men waited in placid silence.

"I hope Silver-Leg has found shelter," one of the men murmured under his breath.

"He should have been here by now," whispered another.

Then they perceived the usual sound of men dismounting, the rattle of chains, the champing of bits, peremptory words of command. Even then they felt that they had nothing to fear: these were all sounds they had heard before. The thicket and the darkness were their allies; they crouched in silence, but they felt that they were safe. Their ears and senses, however, were keenly on the alert: they heard the crackling of dried twigs under the heavy footsteps of the men, the muttered curses that accompanied the struggle against the density of the thicket, the clashing of metal tools against dead branches of intervening trees. Still they did not move. They were not afraid--not yet! But somehow in the obscurity which held them as in a pall their attitude had become more tense, their breathing more laboured, and one or two strong quivering hands went out instinctively to clutch a neighbouring one.

Then suddenly Hare-Lip drew in his breath with a hissing sound like that of an angry snake. He suppressed an imprecation which had forced itself to his lips. Though the almost imperceptible aperture of the burrow he had perceived the flicker of lanthorns: and sounds of broken twigs, of trampling feet, of moving, advancing humanity appeared suddenly to be strangely near.

"By Satan!" he hissed almost inaudibly; "they are in the clearing!"

"They are attacking the thicket," added Mole-Skin in a hoarse whisper.

Never before had the scouring posse of police come so near to the stronghold of these brigands. It was impossible to see how many of them there were, but that they were both numerous and determined could not for a moment be disputed. Voices now became more distinct.

"This way!" "No--that!" "Here, Marcel, where's your pick?" "Lend us your knife, Jules Marie; the bramble has got into my boots."

Some of the men were joking, others swearing lustily. But there were a great number of them, and they were now desperately near.

"They are on us!" came in a husky murmur from Hare-Lip. "They know their way."

"We are betrayed!" was the stifled response.

"By Silver-Leg!" ejaculated Hare-Lip hoarsely, and with such an intensity of vengeful hatred as would have made even the autocratic wooden-legged chief of this band of brigands quake. "The accursed informer! By all the demons in hell he shall pay for his treachery!"

Indeed, there was no longer any doubt that it was not mere chance which was guiding the posse of police to this secret spot. They were making their way unhesitatingly by the dim light of the dark lanterns which their leaders carried before them. One of the men suddenly hit upon the almost imperceptible track, which led straight to the burrow. There was no mistaking the call which he gave to his comrades.

"I have it now, mates!" he shouted. "Follow me!"

The sharp report of a pistol came by way of a reply from the lurking-hole of the Chouans, and the man who had just uttered the call to his mates fell forward on his face.

"Attention, my men!" commanded the officer in charge. "Close the lanterns and put a charge of powder into the brigands' den."

Once more the report of a pistol rang out through the night. But the men of the police, though obviously scared by the mysterious foe who struck at them out of the darkness, were sufficiently disciplined not to give ground: they fought their way into line, and the next moment a terrific volley of gunfire rent the echoes of the wood from end to end. In front of the men now there was a wide clearing, where the undergrowth had been repeatedly broken and trampled upon. This they had seen, just before the lanthorns were closed, and beyond it the burrow with its thatch of heather and its narrow aperture which revealed the muzzle of two or three muskets, and through the aperture several pairs of glowing eyes and shadowy forms vaguely discernible in the gloom.

"Up with the lights and charge!" commanded the officer.

The lanterns were opened, and three sharp reports came in immediate answer from the lair.

One or two men of the police fell amidst the bed of brambles; but the others, maddened by this resistance and by the fall of their comrades, rushed forward in force.

Dividing their line in the centre, they circled round the clearing, attacking the stronghold from two sides. The commissary of police, leaving nothing to chance, had sent half a company to do the work. In a few seconds the men were all over the burrow, scrambling up the thatch, kicking aside the loose walls of dead branches, and within two minutes they had trampled every fragment of the construction under foot.

But of the gang of Chouans there remained only a few traces, and two or three muskets abandoned in their hasty flight: they had succeeded in making good their escape under cover of the darkness. The sergeant in command of the squad of police ordered the débris of the den to be carefully searched. Very little of importance was found beyond a few proofs that the robbery of the mail-coach the other night, the murder of Maxence, and the abortive burglary in Monseigneur's Palace were the work of the same gang.

One or two watches and pocket-books were subsequently identified by the passengers of the coach that had been held up; there was the silver watch which had belonged to the murdered valet, and a couple of books which bore Monseigneur the Bishop of Alençon's bookplate.

But of the man with the wooden leg and his rascally henchmen, or of the sixty-two hundred francs stolen from the coach there was not a sign.

The chief commissary of police swore lustily when his men returned to the bridle-path where he had been waiting for them, and the sergeant reported to him that the rogues had made good their escape. But even his wrath--violent and wordy as it was--was as nothing to the white heat of anger wherewith M. le Procureur Impérial received the news of the dire failure of the midnight raid in the Cache-Renard woods.

Indeed, he appeared so extraordinarily upset at, the time that his subsequent illness was directly attributable to this cause. The leech vowed that his august patient was suffering from a severe shock to his nerves. Be that as it may, M. de Saint-Tropèze, who was usually in such vigorous health, was confined to his room for some days after the raid. It was a fortnight and more ere he again took his walks abroad, as had been his wont in the past, and his friends, when they saw him, could not help but remark that something of M. le Procureur's elasticity and proud bearing had gone. He who used to be so upright now walked with a decided stoop; his face looked at times the colour of ashes; and now and again, when he was out in the streets, he would throw a look around him almost as if he were afraid.

On the other hand, the secret agent of His Imperial Majesty's Police had received the news of the escape of the Chouans with his habitual quietude and equanimity.

He did not make any comment on the commissary's report of the affair, nor did he offer the slightest remonstrance to M. le Procureur Impérial for having permitted the expedition without direct instructions from the official representative of the Minister.

Nothing was seen of the little Man in Grey for the next two or three weeks: he appeared absorbed in the books which M. le préfet so graciously lent him, and he did not trouble either the latter, or M. le Procureur, or the commissary of police with many visits.

The matter of the highway robbery, as well as that of the murdered valet Maxence, appeared to he already relegated to the growing list of the mysterious crimes perpetrated by those atrocious Chouans, with which the police of His Imperial Majesty were unable to cope. The appearance of the enigmatic person in grey had had no deterrent effect on the rascals, nor was it likely to have any, if he proved as inept as the local officials had been in dealing with such flagrant and outrageous felony.

VII

And once again the silence of the forest was broken in the night by the sound of human creatures on the prowl. Through the undergrowth which lies thickest at the Lonrai end of the woods, to the left of the intersecting main road, the measured tread of a footfall could be faintly perceived--it was a strange and halting footfall, as of a man walking with a stump.

Behind the secular willow, which stands in the centre of the small clearing beside the stagnant pool in the very heart of this dense portion of the forest, a lonely watcher crouched, waiting. He had lain there and waited night after night, and for hours at a stretch the surrounding gloom held him in its close embrace: his ears and senses were strained to hear that uneven footfall, whenever its faint thud broke the absolute silence. To no other sound, no other sight, did he pay any attention, or no doubt he would have noticed that in the thicket behind him another watcher cowered. The stalker was stalked in his turn: the watcher was watched. Someone else was waiting in this dense corner for the man with the wooden leg--a small figure rapped in a dark mantle, a silent, furtive creature, more motionless, more noiseless than any beast in its lair.

At last, to-night, that faint, uneven thud of a wooden stump against the soft carpet of the woods reached the straining ears of the two watchers. Anon the feeble flicker of a dark lanthorn was vaguely discernible in the undergrowth.

The man who was crouching behind the willow drew in his breath with a faint, hissing sound; his hand grasped more convulsively the pistol which it held. He was lying flat upon his stomach, like a creeping reptile watching for its prey; his eyes were fixed upon the tiny flickering light as it slowly drew near towards the stagnant pool.

In the thicket behind him the other watcher also lay in wait: his hand, too, closed upon a pistol with a firm and determined grip; the dark mantle slid noiselessly down from his shoulders. But he did not move, and not a twig that helped to give him cover, quivered at his touch.

The next moment a man dressed in a rough blouse and coarse breeches and with a woollen cap pulled over his shaggy hair came out into the clearing. He walked deliberately up to the willow tree. In addition to the small dark lantern which he held in one hand, he carried a spade upon his shoulder. Presently he threw down the spade and then proceeded so to arrange the lantern that its light fell full upon one particular spot, where the dry moss appeared to have been recently disturbed. The man crouching behind the willow watched his every movement; the other behind the thicket hardly dared to breathe.

Then the newcomer did a very curious thing. Sitting down upon the soft, sodden earth, he stretched his wooden stump out before him: it was fastened with straps to the leg which was bent at the knee, the shin and foot beyond appearing like a thick and shapeless mass, swathed with bandages. The supposed maimed man, however, now set to work to undo the straps which bound the wooden stump to his leg, then he removed the stump, straightened out his knee, unwound the few métres of bandages which concealed the shape of his shin and foot, and finally stood up on both legs, as straight and hale as nature had originally made him. The watcher behind the willow had viewed all his movements with tense attention. Now he could scarcely repress a gasp of mingled astonishment and rage, or the vengeful curse which had risen to his lips.

The newcomer took up his spade and, selecting the spot where the moss, and the earth bore traces of having been disturbed, he bent to his task and started to dig. The man behind the tree raised his pistol and fired: the other staggered backwards with a groan--partly of terror and partly of pain--and his left hand went up to his right shoulder with a quick, convulsive gesture. But already the assassin, casting, his still smoking pistol aside, had fallen upon his victim; there was a struggle, brief and grim, a smothered call for help, a savage exclamation of rage and satisfied vengeance, and the wounded man fell at last with a final cry of horror, as his enemy's grip fastened around his throat.

For a second or two the murderer stood quite still contemplating his work. With a couple of vigorous kicks with his boot he turned the body callously over. Then he picked up the lanthorn and allowed the light to play on the dead man's face; he gave one cursory glance at the straight, marble-like features, and at the full, shaggy beard and hair which disfigured the face, and another contemptuous one at the wooden stump which still lay on the ground close by.

"So dies an informer!" he ejaculated with a harsh laugh.

He searched for his pistol and having found it he tucked it into his belt; then putting his fingers to his lips he gave a cry like that of a screech-owl. The cry was answered by a similar one some little distance away; a minute or two later another man appeared through the undergrowth.

"Have you done for him?" queried this stranger in a husky whisper.

"He is dead," replied the other curtly. "Come nearer, Mole-Skin," he added, "you will see something that will amaze you."

Mole-Skin did as his mate ordered; he, too, stood aghast when Hare-Lip pointed to the wooden stump and to the dead man's legs.

"It was not a bad idea!" said Hare-Lip after a while. "It put the police on a wrong scent all the time: while they searched for a man with one leg, he just walked about on two. Silver-Leg was no fool. But," he added savagely, "he was a traitor, and now he'll neither bully nor betray us again."

"What about the money?"

"We'd best get that now. Didn't I tell you that Silver-Leg would come here sooner or later? We lost nothing by lying in wait for him."

Without another word MoleSkin picked up the spade, and in his turn began to dig at the spot where Silver-Leg had toiled when the bullet of his betrayed comrade laid him low. There was only the one spade and Hare-Lip kept watch while his comrade dug. The light from the dark lantern revealed the two miscreants at their work.

While Hare-Lip had thus taken the law into his own hands against the informer, the watcher in the thicket had not stirred. But now he, also, began to crawl slowly and cautiously out of his hiding-place. No snake, or lizard, or crawling, furtive beast could have been more noiseless than he was; the moss beneath him dulled the sound of every movement, till he, too, had reached the willow tree.

The two Chouans were less than. thirty paces away from him. Intent upon their work they had been oblivious of every other sound. Now when the tracker of his human quarry raised his arm to fire, Hare-Lip suddenly turned and at once gave a warning call to his mate. But the call broke upon his lips, there came a sharp report, immediately followed by another--the two brigands, illumined by the lanthorn, had been an easy target, and the hand which wielded the pistol was steady and unerring.

And now stillness more absolute than before reigned in the heart of the forest. Summary justice had been meted out to a base informer by the vengeful arm of the comrades whom he had betrayed, and to the two determined criminals by an equally relentless and retributive hand.

The man who had so inexorably accomplished this last act of unfaltering justice waited for a moment or two until the last lingering echo of the double pistol shot had ceased to resound through the woods. Then he put two fingers to his lips and gave a shrill prolonged whistle; after which he came out from behind the willow. He was small and insignificant-looking, with a pale face and colourless eyes. He was dressed in grey and a grey cap was pulled low down over his forehead. He went up to where the two miscreants whom he had shot were lying, and with a practised eye and hand assured himself that they were indeed dead. He turned the light of the dark lantern first on the man with the queer-shaped lip and then on the latter's companion. The two Chouans had at any rate paid for some of their crimes with their lives; it remained for the Almighty judge to pardon or to punish as they deserved. The third man lay, stark and rigid, where a kick from the other man had roughly cast him aside. His eyes, wide open and inscrutable, had still around them a strange look of authority and pride; the features appeared calm and marble-like; the mouth under the obviously false beard was tightly closed, as if it strove even in death to suppress every sound which might betray the secret that had been so jealously guarded throughout life. Near by lay the wooden stump which had thrown such a cloud of dust into the eyes of good M. Lefèvre and his local police.

With slow deliberation the Man in Grey picked up the wooden stump, and so replaced it against the dead man's leg that in the feeble light and dense black shadows it looked as real as it had done in life--a support for an amputated limb. A moment or two later, the flickering light of a lantern showed through the thicket, and soon the lusty voice of the commissary of police broke in on the watcher's loneliness.

"We heard three distinct shots," explained M. Lefèvre, as soon as he reached the clearing and caught sight of the secret agent.

"Three acts of justice," replied the Man in Grey quietly, as he pointed to the bodies of the three Chouans.

"The man with the wooden leg!" exclaimed the commissary in tones wherein astonishment and unmistakable elation struggled with a momentary feeling of horror. "You have got him?"

"Yes," answered the Man in Grey simply. "Where are your men?"

"I left them at the junction of the bridle-path, as you ordered me to do," growled the commissary sullenly, for he still felt sore and aggrieved at the peremptory commands which had been given to him by the secret agent earlier on that day.

"Then go back and send half a dozen of them here with improvised stretchers to remove the bodies."

"Then it was you, who----" murmured Lefèvre, not knowing, indeed, what to say or do in the face of this puzzling and grim emergency.

"What else would you have had me do?" rejoined the Man in Grey, as, with a steady hand, he removed the false hair and beard which disguised the pale, aristocratic face of M. de Saint-Tropèze.

"Monsieur le Procureur Impérial!" ejaculated Lefèvre hoarsely. "I--I--don't understand--you--you--have killed him--he--oh, my God!"

"The Chouans whom he betrayed killed him, my good Lefèvre," replied the Man in Grey quietly. "He was their chief and kept the secret of his anonymity even from them. When he was amongst them and led them to their many nefarious deeds he was not content to hide his face behind a tangle of false and shaggy hair, or to appear in rough clothes and with grimy hands. No! His artistry in crime went a step farther than that; he strapped a wooden leg to his own whole one and while you scoured the countryside in search of a Chouan with a wooden leg, the latter had resumed his personality as the haughty and well-connected M. de Saint-Tropèze, Procureur at the tribunal of

Alençon to His Majesty the Emperor. Here is the stump," added the Man in Grey, as with the point of his boot he, kicked the wooden stump aside, "and there," he concluded, pointing to the two dead Chouans, "are the men who wreaked their vengeance upon their chief."

"But how----" interjected Lefèvre, who was too bewildered to speak or even to think coherently, "how did you find out--how----"

"Later I may tell you," broke in the Man in Grey shortly, "now we must see to the removal of the bodies. But remember," he added peremptorily and with solemn earnestness, "that everything you have seen and heard to-night must remain for ever a secret within your breast. For the honour of our administration, for the honour of our newly-founded Empire, the dual personality and countless crimes of such a highly placed official as M. de Saint-Tropèze must never be known to the public. I saved the hangman's work when I killed these two men--there is no one living now, save you and I, who can tell the tale of M. de Saint-Tropèze's double entity. Remember that to the public who knew him, to his servants, to your men who will carry his body in all respect and reverence, he has died here by my side in the execution of his duty--disguised in rough clothes in order to help me track these infernal Chouans to their lair. I shall never speak of what I know, and as for you----"

The Man in Grey paused and, even through the gloom, the commissary felt the strength and menace of those colourless eyes fixed steadfastly upon him.

"Your oath, Monsieur le Commissaire de Police," concluded the secret agent in firm, commanding tones.

Awed and subdued--not to say terrified-the chief commissary gave the required oath of absolute secrecy.

"Now go and fetch your men, my good Lefèvre," enjoined the Man in Grey quietly.

Mechanically the commissary turned to go. He felt as if he were in a dream from which he would presently awake. The man whom he had respected and feared, the Procurator of His Majesty the Emperor, whose authority the whole countryside acknowledged, was identical with that nefarious Chouan with the wooden leg whom the entire province loathed and feared.

Indeed, the curious enigma of that dual personality was enough to addle even a clearer intellect than that of the worthy commissary of police. Guided by the light of the lanthorn he carried he made his way back through the thicket whence he had come.

Alone in the forest, the Man in Grey watched over the dead. He looked down meditatively on the pale, aristocratic face of the man who had lied and schemed and planned, robbed and murdered, who had risked so much and committed such villainies, for a purpose which would henceforth and for ever remain an unfathomable mystery.

Was passionate loyalty for the decadent Royalist cause at the root of all the crimes perpetrated by this man of culture and position--or was it merely vulgar greed, vulgar and insatiable worship of money, that drove him to mean and sordid crimes? To what uses did he put the money wrung from peaceable citizens? Did it go to swell the coffers of a hopeless Cause, or to contribute to M. de Saint-Tropèzes own love of luxury?

The Man in Grey pondered these, things in the loneliness and silence of the night. All such questions must henceforth be left unanswered. For the sake of officialdom, of the government of the new Empire, the memory of such a man as M. de Sant-Tropèze must remain for ever untarnished.

Anon the posse of police under the command of a sergeant arrived upon the scene. They had improvised three stretchers; one of these was reverently covered with a mantle, upon which they laid the body of M. le Procureur Impérial, killed in the discharge of his duty whilst aiding to track a gang of desperate Chouans.

VIII

In the forenoon of the following day the chief commissary of Police having seen M. le Préfet on the subject of the arrangements for the public funeral of M. de Saint-Tropèze, called at the lodgings of the secret agent of His Imperial Majesty's Police.

After the usual polite formalities, Lefèvre plunged boldly into the subject of his visit.

"How did you find out?" he asked, trying to carry off the situation with his accustomed bluff. "You owe me an explanation, you know, Monsieur--er--Fernand. I am chief commissary of this district, and by your own statement you stand convicted of having killed two men. Abominable rogues though they were, the laws of France do not allow----"

"I owe you no explanation, my good Lefèvre," interrupted the Man in Grey in his quiet monotone, "as you know. If you would care to take the responsibility on yourself of indicting me for the wilful murder of those two men, you are of course at liberty to do so. But----"

The commissaire hastened to assure the secret emissary of His Majesty that what he had said had only been meant as a joke.

"Only as a spur," he added affably, "to induce you to tell me how you found out the secret of M. de Saint-Tropèze."

"Quite simply," replied the Man in Grey, "by following step by step the series of crimes which culminated in your abortive expedition against the Chouans. On the evening of the attack on the coach on the 10th of October last, I lay hidden and forgotten by the roadside. The coach had driven away; the footpads were making off with their booty. I followed them. I crawled behind them on my hands and knees, till they came to their burrow--the place where you made that foolish and ill-considered attack on them the other night. I heard them quarrelling over their loot; I heard enough to guess that sooner or later a revolt would break out amongst them and that the man whom they called Hare-Lip meant to possess himself of a large share of the spoils. I also heard the man with the wooden leg say something about a book named 'Corinne' which was to be mentioned to 'Monseigneur,' and a key which would be sent to 'Madame' by the intermediary of Red-Poll.

"Within two days of this I learned that a man who had red hair and was valet to Madame la Marquise de Plélan had been murdered, and that a sheet of note-paper covered with random numerals was found upon his person; at the same time a burglary had been committed in the house of Monseigneur the Bishop of Alençon and all that had been stolen were some books. At once I recognised the hand of Hare-Lip and his gang. They had obviously stolen the book from Monseigneur's library and then murdered Red-Poll, in order to possess themselves of the cipher, which I felt sure would prove to be the indication of the secret hiding-place of the stolen booty. It was easy enough to work out the problem of the book and the key. The numerals on the sheet of note-paper referred to pages, lines and words in the book--a clumsy enough cipher at best. It gave me--just as I expected--clear indications of the very place, beside the willow tree and the pool. Also--just as I anticipated--Silver-Leg, the autocratic chief, had in the meanwhile put his threat into execution and punished his rebellious followers by betraying them to the police."

"Great God!" exclaimed Lefèvre, recollecting the anonymous letter which M. le Procureur had handed to him.

"I dare say you recollect this phase of the episode," continued the Man in Grey. "Your expedition against the Chouans nearly upset all my plans. It had the effect of allowing three of them to escape. However, let that pass for the moment. I could not help but guess, when I heard of the attack, that Hare-Lip and his mates would wish to be revenged on the informer. Their burrow was now known to the police, but there was still the hiding-place of the booty, to which sooner or later I knew that Silver-Leg must return.

"You remember the orders I gave you a full month ago; to be prepared to go on any day and at an instant's notice with a dozen of your men to a certain point on the main road at the Lonrai end of the wood which I had indicated to you, whenever I sent you a peremptory message to do so, and there to wait in silence and on the alert until a shrill whistle from me brought you to my side. Well! in this matter you did your duty well, and the Minister shall hear of it.

"As for me, I was content to bide my time. With the faithful henchman whom you placed at my disposal I lay in wait for Monsieur de Saint-Tropèze in the Rue St. Blaise during all those weary days and nights when he was supposed to be too ill to venture out of his house. At last he could refrain no longer; greed or perhaps sheer curiosity, or that wild adventurous spirit which made him what he was, drove him to lend a deaf ear to the dictates of prudence and to don once again the shaggy beard, the rough clothes and wooden stump of his lawless and shady life.

"I had so placed your man that from where he was he could not see Monsieur le Procureur, whenever the latter came out of his house, nor did he know whom or what it was that I was watching; but as soon as I saw Monsieur de Saint-Tropèze emerging stealthily from his side gate, I dispatched your man to you with the peremptory message to go at once to the appointed place, and then I started in the wake of my quarry.

"You, my good Lefèvre, have no conception what it means to track--unseen and unheard--one of those reckless Chouans who are more alert than any wild beast. But I tracked my man; he came out of his house when the night was at its darkest and first made his way to that small derelict den which no doubt you know and which stands just off the main road, on the fringe of the Cache-Renard wood. This he entered and came out about a quarter of an hour later, dressed in his Chouan rig-out. I must own that for a few seconds he almost deceived me, so marvellous was his disguise; the way he contrived that wooden leg was positively amazing.

"After that he plunged into the woods. But I no longer followed him; I knew whither he was going and was afraid lest, in the depths and silence of the forest, he would hear my footfall and manage to give me the slip. Whilst he worked his way laboriously with his wooden stump through the thicket and the undergrowth, I struck boldly along the main road, and plunged into the wood at the point which had been revealed to me by the cipher. I had explored the place many a time during the past month, and had no difficulty in finding the stagnant pool and the willow tree. Hare-Lip and his mate were as usual on the watch. No sooner had Silver-Leg appeared on the scene than the others meted out to him the full measure of their vengeful justice. But I could not allow them to be, taken alive. I did not know how much they knew or guessed of their leader's secret, or how much they might reveal at their first interrogation. The gallows had already claimed them for its own; for me they were a facile prey. I shot them both deliberately and will answer to His Majesty's Minister of Police alone for my actions."

The Man in Grey paused. As he completed his narrative Lefèvre stared at him, dumbfounded at the courage, the determination, the dogged perseverance which alone could have brought this amazing undertaking to its grim and gruesome issue.

"After this, my good Lefèvre," remarked the secret agent more lightly, "we shall have to find out something about 'Madame' and quite a good deal about 'Monseigneur.'"

II. THE SPANIARD

I

THE man with the wooden leg was still at large, and M. le Procureur Impérial had died a hero's death whilst helping to capture a gang of desperate Chouans in the Cache-Renard woods. This was the public version of the tragic epilogue to those three mysteries, which had puzzled and terrified the countryside during the early days of October, 1809--the robbery of the mail-coach, the burglary in the Palace of Monseigneur the Constitutional Bishop of Alençon, and the murder of Mme. Marquise de Plélan's Valet, Maxence.

The intelligent section of the public was loud in its condemnation of the ineptitude displayed by the police in the matter of those abominable crimes, and chief commissary Lefèvre, bound by oath--not to say terror--to hold his tongue as to the real facts of the case, grumbled in his beard and muttered curses on the accredited representative of the Minister of Police--ay, and on M. le Duc d'Otrante himself.

On top of all the public unrest and dissatisfaction came the outrage at the house of M. de Kerblay, a noted advocate of the Paris bar and member of the Senate, who owned a small property in the neighbourhood of Alençon, where he spent a couple of months every year with his wife and family, entertaining a few friends during the shooting season.

In the morning of November the 6th, the neighbourhood was horrified to hear that on the previous night, shortly after ten o'clock, a party of those ruffianly Chouans had made a descent on M. de Kerblay's house, Les Ormeaux. They had demanded admittance in the name of the law. All the servants had gone to bed with the exception of Hector, M. de Kerblay's valet, and he was so scared that he allowed the scélérats to push their way into the house, before he had realised who they were. Ere he could call for help he was set upon, gagged, and locked up in his pantry. The Chouans then proceeded noiselessly upstairs. Mme. de Kerblay was already in bed. The Senator was in his dressing-room, half undressed.

They took him completely by surprise, held a pistol to his head, and demanded the immediate payment of twenty-five thousand francs. Should the Senator summon his servants, the rogues would shoot him and his wife and even his children summarily, if they were stopped in their purpose or hindered in their escape.

M. de Kerblay was considerably over sixty. Not too robust in health, terrorised and subdued, he yielded, and with the muzzle of a pistol held to his head and half a dozen swords gleaming around him, he produced the keys of his secrétaire and handed over to the Chouans not only all the money he had in the house--something over twenty thousand francs--but a diamond ring, valued at another twenty thousand, which had been given to him by the Emperor in recognition of signal services rendered in the matter of the affairs of the ex-Empress.

Whereupon the wretches departed as silently as they had come, and by the time the hue and cry was raised they had disappeared, leaving no clue or trace.

The general consensus of opinion attributed the outrage to the man with the wooden leg. M. Lefèvre, chief commissary of police, who knew that that particular scoundrel was reposing in the honoured vault of the Saint-Tropèze family, was severely nonplussed. Since the sinister episode of the dual personality of M. de Saint-Tropèze he realised more than ever how difficult it was to deal with these Chouans. Here to-day, gone to-morrow, they were veritable masters in the art of concealing their identity, and in this quiet corner of Normandy it was impossible to shake a man by the hand without wondering whether he did not perchance belong to that secret gang of malefactors.

M. de Kerblay, more distressed at the loss of his ring than of his money, offered a reward of five thousand francs for its recovery; but while M. Lefèvre's zeal was greatly stimulated thereby, the Man in Grey appeared disinclined to move in the matter, and his quiet, impassive attitude grated unpleasantly on the chief commissary's feelings.

About a week after the outrage, on a cold, wet morning in November, M. Lefèvre made a tempestuous irruption into the apartments in the Rue de France occupied by the secret agent of the Minister of Police.

"We hold the ruffians!" he cried, waving his arm excitedly. "That's the best of those scoundrels! They are always quarrelling among themselves! They lie and they cheat and betray one another into our hands!"

The Man in Grey, as was his wont, waited patiently until the flood of M. Lefèvre's impassioned eloquence had somewhat subsided, then he said quietly:

"You have had the visit of an informer?"

"Yes," replied the Commissary, as he sank, panting, into a chair.

"A man you know?"

"By sight. Oh, one knows those rogues vaguely. One sees them about one day--they disappear the next--they have their lairs in the most inaccessible corners of this cursed country. Yes! I know the man by sight. He passed through my hands into the army a year ago. A deserter, of course. Though his appearance does not tally with any of the descriptions we have received from the Ministry of War, we know that these fellows have a way of altering even their features on occasions, and this man has 'deserter' written all over his ugly countenance."

"Well! And what has he told you?"

"That he will deliver to us the leader of the gang who broke into Monsieur de Kerblay's house the other night."

"On conditions, of course."

"Of course."

"Immunity for himself?"

"Yes."

"And a reward?"

"Yes."

"You did not agree to that, I hope," said the Man in Grey sternly.

M. Lefèvre hummed and hawed.

"There must be no question of bribing these men to betray one another," resumed the secret agent firmly, "or you'll be falling into one baited trap after another."

"But there's Monsieur de Kerblay's offer of a reward for the recovery of the ring, and in this case----" protested Lefèvre sullenly.

"In no case," broke in the Man in Grey.

"Then what shall I do with the man?"

"Promise him a free pardon for himself and permission to rejoin his regiment if his information proves to be correct. Keep him in the police-cells, and come and report to me directly you have extracted from him all he knows, or is willing to tell."

The chief commissary of police was well aware that when the Minister's secret agent assumed that quiet air of authority, neither argument nor resistance was advisable. He muttered something between his teeth, but receiving no further response from the Man in Grey he turned abruptly on his heel and stalked out of the room, murmuring inaudible things about "officiousness" and "incompetence."

II

The man who had presented himself that morning at the commissariat of police offering valuable information as to the whereabouts of the leaders of his own gang, appeared as the regular type of the unkempt, out-at-elbows down-at-heels, unwashed Chouan who had of a truth become the pest and terror of the countryside. He wore a long shaggy beard, his hair was matted and tousled his blouse and breeches were in rags, and his bare feet were thrust into a pair of heavy leather shoes. During his brief sojourn in the army, or in the course of his subsequent lawless life, he had lost one eye, and the terrible gash across that part of his face gave his countenance a peculiarly sinister expression.

He stood before the commissary of police, twirling a woollen cap between his grimy fingers, taciturn sullen and defiant.

"I'll say nothing," he repeated for the third time, "unless I am paid to speak."

"You are amenable to the law, my man," said the chief commissary dryly. "You'll be shot, unless you choose to earn a free pardon for yourself by making a frank confession of your misdeeds."

"And what's a free pardon to me," retorted the Chouan roughly, "if I am to starve on it?"

"You will be allowed to at once rejoin your regiment."

"Bah!"

The man spat on the ground, by way of expressing his contempt at the prospect.

"I'd as lief be shot at once," he declared emphatically.

M. Lefèvre could have torn his scanty hair with rage. He was furious with the Chouan and his obstinacy, and furious with that tiresome man in the grey coat who lorded it over every official in the district, and assumed an authority which he ought never to have been allowed to wield.

The one-eyed Chouan was taken back to the police-cells, and M. Lefèvre gave himself over to his gloomy meditations. Success and a goodly amount of credit--not to mention the five thousand francs' reward for the recovery of the ring--appeared just within his reach. A couple of thousand francs out of the municipal funds to that wretched informer, and the chiefs of one of the most desperate gangs of

Chouans would fall into M. Lefèvre's hands, together with no small measure of glory for the brilliant capture. It was positively maddening!

It was not till late in the afternoon that the worthy commissary had an inspiration--such a grand one that he smacked his high forehead, marvelling it had not come to him before. What were two thousand francs out of his own pocket beside the meed of praise which would fall to his share, if he succeeded in laying one or two of those Chouan leaders by the heels? He need not touch the municipal funds. He had a couple of thousand francs put by and more; and, surely, that sum would be a sound investment for future advancement and the recognition of his services on the part of the Minister himself, in addition to which there would be his share in M. de Kerblay's reward.

So M. Lefèvre sent for the one-eyed Chouan and once more interrogated him, cajoling and threatening alternately, with a view to obtaining gratis the information which the man was only prepared to sell.

"I'll say nothing," reiterated the Chouan obstinately, "unless I am paid to speak."

"Well! What will you take?" said the commissary at last.

"Five thousand francs," replied the man glibly.

"I'll give you one," rejoined M. Lefèvre. "But mind," he added with uncompromising severity, "you remain here in the cells as hostage for your own good faith. If you lie to me, you will be shot--summarily and without trial."

"Give me three thousand and I'll speak," said the Chouan.

"Two thousand," rejoined the commissary, "and that is my last word."

For a second or two the man appeared to hesitate; with his one eye he tried to fathom the strength of M. le Commissaire's determination. Then he said abruptly:

"Very well, I'll take two thousand francs. Give me the money now and I'll speak."

Without another superfluous word M. Lefèvre counted out twenty one-hundred franc notes, and gave them into the Chouan's grimy hand. He thought it best to appear open-handed and to pay cash down; the man would be taken straight back to the cells presently, and if he played a double game he would anyhow forfeit the money together with his life.

"Now," said Lefèvre as soon as the man had thrust the notes into the pocket of his breeches, "tell me who is your chief, and where a posse of my police can lay hands upon him."

"The chief of my gang," rejoined the Chouan, "is called 'the Spaniard' amongst us; his real name is Carrera and he comes from Madrid. We don't often see him, but it was he who led the expedition to the house of Monsieur de Kerblay."

"What is he like?"

"A short man with dark, swarthy skin, small features, keen, jet-black eyes, no lashes, and very little eyebrow, a shock of coal-black hair and a square black beard and moustache; he speaks French with a Spanish accent."

"Very good! Now tell me where we can find him."

"At Chéron's farm on the Chartres road between la Mesle and Montagne. You know it?"

"I know the farm. I don't know Chéron. Well?"

"The Spaniard has arranged to meet a man there--a German Jew--while Chéron himself is away from home. The idea is to dispose of the ring."

"I understand. When is the meeting to take place?"

"To-night! It is market day at Chartres and Chéron will be absent two days. It was all arranged yesterday. The Spaniard and his gang will sleep at the farm; the following morning they will leave for Paris, en route some of them, so 'tis said, for Spain."

"And the farmer--Chéron? What has he to do with it all?"

"Nothing," replied the Chouan curtly. "He is just a fool. His house stands isolated in a lonely part of the country, and his two farm hands are stupid louts. So, whenever the Spaniard wants to meet any of his accomplices privately, he selects a day when Chéron is from home, and makes use of the farm for his own schemes."

"You owe him a grudge, I suppose," sneered Lefèvre, who had taken rapid notes of all the man had told him.

"No," replied the Chouan slowly, "but those of us who helped to work the coup at Monsieur de Kerblay's the other night, were each to receive twenty francs as our share of the spoils. It was not enough!"

The commissary of police nodded complacently. He was vastly satisfied with the morning's work. He had before now heard vague hints about this Spaniard, one of those mysterious and redoubtable Chouan leaders, who had given the police of the entire province no end of trouble and grave cause for uneasiness. Now by his--Lefèvre's--own astuteness he stood not only to lay the villain by the heels and earn commendation for his zeal from the Minister himself, but, if this one-eyed scoundrel spoke the truth, also to capture some of his more prominent accomplices, not to mention the ring and M. de Kerblay's generous reward.

Incidentally he also stood to put a spoke in the wheel of that over-masterful and interfering man in the grey coat, which would be a triumph not by any means to be depreciated.

So the Chouan was taken back to the cells and the chief commissary of police was left free to make his arrangements for the night's expedition, without referring the matter to the accredited agent of His Majesty's Police.

III

Lefèvre knew that he was taking a grave risk when, shortly after eight o'clock on that same evening, he ordered a squadron of his police to follow him to Chéron's farm on the Chartres road. At the last moment he even had a few misgivings as to the wisdom of his action. If the expedition did not meet with the measure of success which he anticipated, and the accredited agent of the Minister came to hear of it, something exceedingly unpleasant to the over-zealous commissary might be the result. However, after a few very brief moments of this unworthy hesitation, M. Lefèvre chid himself for his cowardice and started on his way.

Since his interview with the one-eyed Chouan he had been over to the farm in order to get a thorough knowledge of the topography of the buildings and of their surroundings. Disguised as a labourer he had hung about the neighbourhood, in the wet and cold until he felt quite sure that he could find his way anywhere around the place in the dark.

The farm stood a couple of kilomètres or so from the road, on the bank of a tiny tributary of the Mayenne, surrounded by weeping willows, now stripped of their leaves, and flanked by a couple of tumble-down heather-thatched sheds. It was a square building, devoid of any outstanding architectural features, and looking inexpressibly lonely and forlorn. There was not another human habitation in sight, and the wooded heights which dominated the valley appeared to shut the inhabitants of the little farm away from the rest of mankind. As he looked at the vast and mournful solitude around, Lefèvre easily recognised how an astute leader, such as the Spaniard appeared to be, would choose it as headquarters for his schemes. Whenever the house itself became unsafe the thicket of willow and chestnut close by, and the dense undergrowth on the heights above, would afford perfect shelter for fugitive marauders.

It was close on ten o'clock of an exceptionally dark night when the posse of police, under the command of the chief commissary, dismounted at the "Grand Duc," a small wayside inn on the Chartres road, and, having stabled their horses, started on foot across country at the heels of their chief. The earth was sodden with recent rains and the little troop moved along in silence, their feet, encased in shoes of soft leather, making no sound as they stealthily advanced.

The little rivulet wound its sluggish course between flat banks bordered by waste land on either side. Far ahead a tiny light gleamed intermittently, like a will-o'-the-wisp, as intervening groups of trees alternately screened it and displayed it to view.

After half an hour of heavy walking the commissary called a halt. The massive block of the farmhouse stood out like a dense and dark mass in the midst of the surrounding gloom. M. Lefèvre called softly to his sergeant.

"Steal along, Hippolyte," he whispered, "under cover of those willow trees, and when you hear me give the first command to open, surround the house so that the rascals cannot escape either by the door or the windows."

Silently and noiselessly these orders were executed; whilst the commissary himself stole up to the house. He came to a halt before the front door and paused a moment, peering anxiously round about him and listening for any sound which might come from within. The house appeared dark and deserted; only from one of the windows on the ground floor a feeble light filtered through the chinks of an ill-fitting shutter, and a mingled murmur of voices seemed to travel thence intermittently. But of this the eager watcher could not be sure. The north-westerly wind, soughing through the bare branches of the trees behind him, also caused the shutters to creak on their hinges and effectually confused every other sound.

The chief commissary then rapped vigorously against the door with the hilt of his sword.

"Open!" he called peremptorily, "in the name of the law!"

Already he could hear the sergeant and his men stealing out from under the trees; but from the stronghold of the Chouans there came no answer to his summons; absolute silence reigned inside the farmhouse; the dismal creaking of a half-broken shutter and the murmur of the wind in the leafless willows alone roused the dormant echoes of the old walls.

Lefèvre rapped once more against the massive panels.

"Open!" he called again, "in the name of the law!"

The men following their sergeant had now reached the open. In an instant, from somewhere in the gloom behind them, there came the report of two musket shots in rapid succession. Someone was hit, for there was the sound of a groan and a curse; but in the darkness it was impossible to see who it was.

The men halted irresolute.

"Run to the back of the house, some of you!" commanded the commissary, "and in Heaven's name do not allow a single ruffian to escape."

The men obeyed as quickly as the darkness would allow, and again two musket shots rang out from among the trees; this time the sergeant fell forward on his face.

"Corporal Crosnier, are you there?" cried Commissary Lefèvre.

"Present, my commandant!" was the quick reply.

"Take Jean Marie and Dominique and two or three others with you, and put up the game that is lurking under those willows."

Crosnier obeyed; he called half a dozen men to him and marched them up towards the thicket. The cowering enemy lay low; only from time to time shots rang out simultaneously out of the darkness. Sometimes they made a hit, but not often--one or two of the men received a stray bullet in their shoulder or their leg--a random shot which came from out of the gloom and to which they could not reply, for it was impossible to see whence it had come. Presently even that intermittent fire ceased. It seemed as if the thicket had finally swallowed up the lurking quarry.

In the meantime Lefèvre had ordered two or three of his picked men to use the butt-end of their muskets against the door.

"Batter it in, my men," he commanded, "and arrest everyone you find inside the house."

Strangely enough, considering the usually desperate tactics of these Chouan gangs when brought to bay, no resistance was offered from the interior of their stronghold. Whether the rascals were short of ammunition and were saving it for a hand-to-hand fight later, or whether they were preparing some bold coup, it was impossible to say. Certain it is that the vigorgus attacks against the front door were met by absolute silence--so absolute, indeed, as vaguely to disconcert the commissary of police.

Still the men continued to pound away with their muskets against the panels of the door; but the latter was extraordinarily massive in comparison with the want of solidity of the rest of the house. It resisted every onslaught for some time, until at last it fell in with a terrific crash, and Lefèvre, leaving half a dozen men on guard outside, took another half-dozen with him and entered.

He had picked his men from among those whom he knew to be most intrepid, for he had expected a desperate resistance on the part of the Chouans; he was prepared to be greeted with a volley of musket-fire as he and his men crossed the threshold; he was prepared for a hand-to-hand fight across that battered door. In fact, M. Lefèvre, chief commissary of police, had been prepared for everything excepting the death-like stillness which he encountered by way of welcome.

Darkness and silence held undisputed sway everywhere. The men, with dark lanterns fixed to their belts and holding loaded muskets in their hands, paused for one moment irresolute. Then they started to make a thorough search of the place; first the ground floor, then the entrance hall and staircase, then the cellars. They explored every nook and cranny where human quarry might find shelter, but there was not a sign, hardly a trace of any Chouans, save in one small room on the ground floor which certainly appeared as if it had been recently occupied; the chairs had been hastily pushed aside, on the centre table were half a dozen mugs and two or three jugs, one of which was still half filled with wine, a handful of ashes smouldered in the hearth, and the lamp which hung from the ceiling above was alight. But for this, Lefèvre might have thought that he must have been dreaming when he stood by the front door and saw the narrow stream of light through the chink of a shutter.

Indeed, there was something unspeakably dreary and desolate in this dark and empty house, in which undoubtedly a gang of malefactors had lately held revel; and when the men went upstairs in order to explore the floor above, they were, every one of them, conscious of the quick sense of unreasoning terror when a weird and intermittent sound suddenly reached their ear.

The sound came from over their heads--it was like a wail, and was piteous and disconcerting in the extreme.

"Like someone groaning," said one of the men in a hoarse whisper.

Soon their momentary feeling of dread passed away, and two or three of the men had already scaled the narrow, ladder-like stairs which led to a loft that ran the whole length and breadth of the house under the sloping roof.

But here an extraordinary sight met their gaze. Huddled up against a large supporting beam were an old man, a woman and two young girls. They had been tied together by ropes to the beam. Each of the unfortunates was in acute distress or bodily pain. The atmosphere of the place was both stuffy and bitterly cold. Incessant moaning came from the woman, sobbing from the girls; the man appeared stunned and dazed. When the light from one of the dark lanterns fell upon him, he blinked his eyes and gazed vacantly on the men who were already busy with the ropes, freeing him and the woman from their bonds.

They all appeared in the last stage of exhaustion and clung to one another for support and warmth, when Lefèvre with kindly authority ordered them to move. Fortunately one of the men recollected the jug of wine which had been left in the room on the ground floor. He ran to fetch it, and returned very soon jug and glasses in hand. In the meanwhile Lefèvre had remained staring at the wretched people and trying to extract a few words of explanation from them.

So far he had only been able to elicit the information that four members of the farmer Chéron's family, his father, his wife and his two daughters stood before him in this pitiable plight. It was only after they had drunk a little wine that they were able to speak coherently. In short, jerky sentences and with teeth still chattering with cold and terror, the old man tried to reply to the commissary's questions.

"How in the world came you to be up here," M. Lefèvre asked, "tied like cattle to a beam in your son's house?"

"My son is away at Chartres, Monsieur le Commissaire," replied the old man; "he won't return till to-morrow. We should have perished of hunger and cold if you had not come to our rescue."

"But where are those blackguardly Chouans? And who in the devil's name fired on us from under your trees?"

"Those execrable Chouans took possession of my son's house this morning, Monsieur le Commissaire, soon after his departure," answered the old man dolefully. "They seized me and my daughter-in-law and my two grandchildren, forced us to give up the little bit of money which my son had left for our use, stole food from the larder and wine from the cellar; and when we protested they dragged us up here--as you say--like cattle, tied us to a beam and left us to perish unless my son should chance to come home."

Lefèvre would have liked to say that twenty-four hours spent in a draughty loft does not necessarily mean starvation, but on the whole he refrained from badgering the poor people, who had suffered quite enough, with further expostulation.

"But what has happened to the Chouans?" he reiterated with a hearty curse.

"Gone, Monsieur le Commissaire," here interposed the woman woefully. "Gone! They caroused all day, and left about a couple of hours ago; since then the house has been as silent as the grave."

Lefèvre said nothing very coherent for the moment; he was mentally embracing the Chouans, the lying informer and his own folly in one comprehensive curse.

"But my men were fired on from behind the trees," he urged feebly after a while.

"I heard the firing, too, Monsieur le Commissaire," rejoined the old man. "It terrified us, for the Chouans had threatened to shoot us all if they were attacked by the police; and these two young girls--think of it, Monsieur le Commissaire at the mercy of those brutes. I suppose," he added with a shudder, "that while the leaders of the gang made good their escape, they left a couple of men behind to cover their retreat."

Nothing more could, be got out of these poor people. They had been set upon quite early in the day by the Chouans, and knew little or nothing of what had gone on in the house while they were prisoners in the loft. They did not know how many of the ruffians there were--six or eight they thought. The chief was a man with swarthy skin and a long black beard, who spoke French with a strange foreign accent.

The commissary of police went nearly mad with rage. He set his best men to search the farm-house through and through, in the hope that some of the rascals might still be lurking about the place. But the men ransacked the house in vain. They found neither trap-door nor secret panel, nor slinking quarry, and after a couple of hours' hunt were forced to own themselves defeated.

IV

M. Lefèvre returned to Alençon with his posse of police in the small hours of the morning. He dismissed the men at the commissariat, and sought his own lodgings in the Rue Notre Dame, his mind a prey to the bitterest feeling of disappointment--not unmixed with misgivings at thought of M. le Ministre's agent, should he get wind of the miscarriage.

To his terror and amazement, no sooner had he entered the house than the concierge came out of his lodge to tell him that a gentleman was upstairs in his rooms, waiting for him.

"Who is it?" he asked sharply. "You have no right to admit anyone to my rooms at this hour of the night."

"I could not help myself," retorted the concierge sullenly. "He exhibited some sort of order from the Ministry of Police, and was so high-handed and peremptory that I dared not refuse."

Filled with vague apprehension M. Lefèvre ran quickly up to his rooms. He was greeted in the ante-chamber by the Man in Grey.

"I was unfortunately too late to catch you before you started," said the latter as soon as Lefèvre had closed the door. He spoke in his even monotone--his face was calm and expressionless, but there was something about his attitude which jarred unpleasantly on the commissary's nerves.

"I--that is----" he stammered, despite his stern effort to appear confident and at his ease.

"You have disobeyed the Minister's orders," interposed the secret agent quietly. "But there is no time now to discuss your conduct. The blunder which you have just committed is mayhap, beyond repair; in which case----"

He broke off abruptly and M. Lefèvre felt a cold shiver running down his spine.

"There was no time to consult you----" he began.

"I said that I would not discuss that," interposed the Man in Grey quietly. "Tell me where you have been!"

"To Chéron's farm on the Chartres road," replied the commissary sullenly.

"The informer gave you directions?"

"Yes."

"That you would find his leader there?"

"Yes, the man whom they call 'the Spaniard,' and some of his accomplices. The informer----"

"The informer escaped from the cells during your absence this evening," said the Man in Grey curtly.

"Malediction!"

"Do not curse, my good man," advised the other dryly. "The rascal's escape may be the means of retrieving your blunder, since it gave me the knowledge of the whole affair."

"But how did it happen?"

"Surveillance slackened while you went off on your wild-goose chase. Your prisoner used some of the money wherewith you had bribed him--against my express command, remember--to bribe his warder in his turn. Your sergeant-in-charge came to me in his distress when he found that his bird had flown."

Lefèvre had no longer the strength to argue or even to curse. He hung his head in silent dejection.

"I sent for you," continued the Man in Grey mercilessly. "When I found that you had gone no one knew whither, and that you had taken a posse of your men with you, I guessed the whole extent of your damnable blunder. I have waited here for you ever since."

"What can I do now?" murmured Lefèvre gloomily.

"Collect ten or twelve of the men whom you can most confidently trust, and then pick me up at my lodgings in the Rue de France. We'll go back to Chéron's farm--together."

"But there is no one there," said Lefèvre with a dejected sigh, "only Chéron's father, his wife and two daughters."

"I know that well enough, you fool," exclaimed the Man in Grey, departing for the first time from his habitual calm, and starting to pace up and down the narrow room like a caged and fretting animal; "and that every proof against the villains who robbed Monsieur de Kerblay has no doubt vanished whilst you were getting the wrong sow by the car. To bring the crime home to them now will he very difficult. 'Tis red-handed we ought to have caught them, with the Jew there and the ring and the Spaniard bargaining, whereas now----"

Suddenly he paused and stood quite still; the anger and impatience died out of his face, leaving it pale and expressionless as was its wont; only to Lefèvre who was watching him with keen anxiety it seemed as if for one fraction of a second a curious glitter had lit up his colourless eyes.

"In Heaven's name!" he resumed impatiently after a while, "let us get to horse, or I may be tempted, to tell you what I think of your folly."

The commissary, trounced like a recalcitrant schoolboy and not a little terrified at the consequences of his blunder, was only too ready to obey. Within half an hour he was in the saddle. He had Corporal Crosnier with him and half a dozen picked men, and together they went to the Rue de France where the Minister's agent was waiting for them.

V

It was close upon five o'clock of a raw, damp morning when the little party drew rein once more at the wayside inn on the Chartres road. The men appeared tired out and were grateful for the hot coffee which a sleepy ostler hastily prepared for them; but the Man in Grey seemed indefatigable. Wrapped to the chin in a long, dark mantle, he had ridden the whole way by the side of the commissary, plying him with questions the while. Bit by bit he had extracted from him the full history of the futile expedition, the description of the house, its situation and structure, and of the members of the Chéron family. Now, whilst sipping his coffee, he made Lefèvre give him final and minute directions how to reach the farm-house.

Ten minutes later he started on his way--alone and on foot.

"Follow me in about five minutes," were his last commands to the commissary. "Then lie low under the trees. When you hear a pistol shot from inside the house rush in and seize every man, woman, or child whom you find; if you meet with any resistance order your men to use their muskets. Leave the Corporal with a strong guard outside the house, both back and front, and bid him shoot on sight anyone who attempts to escape."

After he had walked on through the darkness for a couple of mètres or so, he threw off his mantle and hat and kicked off his shoes. The commissary of police, had he been near him now, would of a truth have been staggered at his appearance. He wore a pair of ragged breeches and a stained and tattered blouse; his hair was unkempt, and his feet and legs were bare to the knees.

"Now for a little bit of luck," he murmured as he started to run. His bare feet squelched through the wet earth and spattered him with mud from head to foot, and as he ran the perspiration streamed down his face and mingled with the grime. Indeed, it seemed as if he took a special delight in tiring himself out, in getting breathless and hot, and by his active exercise making himself look even dirtier and more disreputable than he had been before.

When he reached the river side and the row of willow trees, he halted; the house, he knew, must be quite close now on the right, and as he peered into the darkness he perceived a tiny streak of light glimmering feebly through the gloom some way off. Throwing himself flat upon his stomach, he bent his ear to the ground; it was attuned to the slightest sound, like that of the Indian trackers, and he heard at a distance of four hundred mètres behind him the measured tramp of Lefèvre's men. Then he rose to his feet and, stealthily as a cat, crept up to the house.

The slender streak of light guided him and, as he drew nearer, he heard a confused murmur of voices raised in merriment. The occupants of the house were apparently astir; the light came through a half-open shutter on the ground floor as did the sound of the voices, through which presently there rang a loud and prolonged peal of laughter. The secret agent drew a deep sigh of satisfaction; the birds--thank goodness--had not yet flown. Noiselessly he approached the front door, the battered and broken appearance of which bore testimony to Lefèvre's zeal.

A bright patch of light striking through an open door on the right illumined a portion of the narrow hall beyond, leaving the rest in complete darkness. The Man in Grey stepped furtively over the threshold. Immediately he was challenged: "Who goes there?" and he felt rather than saw a gun levelled at his head.

"A friend," he murmured timidly.

At the instant the challenge had resounded through the house the light in the inner room on the right was suddenly extinguished; deathly silence had succeeded the debauch.

"What's your business?" queried a muffled voice peremptorily.

Before the Man in Grey could reply there was a commotion in the inner room as of chairs hastily thrust aside, and presently another voice--one both gruff and commanding--called out: "What is it, Pierre?"

A dark lantern was flashed about, its light fell full on the miserable apparition of the Man in Grey.

"What do you want?" queried the commanding voice out of the partial gloom. "Speak, or I fire!"

"A friend!" reiterated the Man in Grey timidly.

"Your name?"

"Nicaise, sir, from Mauger's farm on the Mayenne road. I was asleep under a haystack, when a stranger comes to me and shakes me roughly by the shoulder. 'Run,' he says to me, 'to Chéron's up by the Chartres road. Run as fast as your legs will take you. Walk in boldly; the door is open. You will find company inside the farm. Tell them the police are coming back in force. Someone will give you a silver franc for your pains if you get there in time.' So I took to my heels and ran."

While he spoke another man and a woman had entered. Their vague forms were faintly discernible through the darkness; the light from the lantern still struck full on the Man in Grey, who looked the picture of woebegone imbecility.

From the group in the doorway there came a murmur: "The police!"

"A stranger, you say?" queried the man with the commanding voice. "What was he like?"

"I could not say," replied the secret agent humbly. "It was very dark. But he said I should get a silver franc for my pains, and I am a poor man. I thought at first it was a hoax, but when I crossed the meadow just now I saw a lot of men in hiding under the willow trees."

"Malediction!" muttered the man, as he turned, undecided, towards his companions. "Oh, that I had that one-eyed traitor in my power!" he added with a savage oath.

"Did you speak to the men of the police?" asked a woman's voice out of the darkness.

"No, madame," replied the secret agent. "They did not see me. I was crawling on my hands and knees. But they are all round the house, and I heard one man calling to the sergeant and giving him orders to watch the doors and windows lest anyone tried to escape."

The group in the doorway was silent; the man who had been on guard appeared to have joined them, and they all went back into the room and held a hurried consultation.

"There is nothing for it," said one man, "but to resume our former rôles as members of the Chéron family, and to do it as naturally as before."

"They suspect us now," said another, "or they would not he here again so soon."

"Even so; but if we play our parts well they can only take us back to the commissariat and question us; they must release us in the end; they have no proof."

In the meanwhile someone had relighted the lamp. There appeared to be a good deal of scurrying and scrambling inside the room; the Man in Grey tiptoed up to the doorway to see what was going on. Evidently, disguises which had hastily been put aside had been resumed; the group stood before him now just as Lefèvre had originally described them: the old man, the woman, the two young girls; the latter were striding about the room and holding their skirts up clumsily with both hands, as men are wont to do when they don women's clothes; the old man, on whom grey locks and well-stencilled wrinkles were the only signs of age, was hastily putting these to rights before a mirror on the wall.

But it was the woman's doings which compelled the attention of the Man in Grey. She was standing on a chair with her back to him, intent on manipulating something up the huge open chimney.

"It will be quite safe there," she said.

She appeared to he closing some heavy iron door which fell in its place with a snap. Then she turned to her companions and slowly descended from the chair. "When the present storm has blown over," she said, "we'll come and fetch it. Chéron will never guess; at any rate, we are sure the police cannot discover this most excellent hiding-place."

She was a short, square-built woman, with a dark, almost swarthy skin, keen jet-black eyes which appeared peculiarly hard and glittering owing to the absence of lashes, a firm, thin-lipped mouth, square chin, and low forehead crowned by a shock of thick, black hair cut short like a boy's. The secret agent kept his eyes fixed upon her while she spoke to her friends. He noted the head so full of character, and the strength and determination expressed in every line of the face; he marvelled why the features--especially those glittering jet-black eyes--appeared familiar, as something he had known and heard of before. And, suddenly, it all came to him in a flash; he remembered the informer's description of the leader named "the Spaniard": a dark, swarthy skin, jet-black hair, keen dark eyes with no lashes to soften their glitter, the beard, the man's attire, the foreign accent. Soh! these marauding Chouans slipped in and out of their disguises and changed even their sex outwardly as easily as men change their coats; whilst the very identity of their leader was more often unknown to them than known.

As the secret agent's practised glance took in during these few seconds the whole personality of the woman before him, he knew that his surmises--based on intuition and on reasoning--were correct. It was the Spaniard who stood before him now, but the Spaniard was a woman. And as he gazed on her, half in pity because of her sex, and half in admiration for her intrepidity, she turned, and their glances met. She looked at him across the narrow room, and each knew that the other had guessed.

The woman never flinched; she held the agent's glance and did not utter either word or cry whilst with a slow, deliberate movement, she drew a pistol from beneath her kerchief. But he, as quick and resourceful, had instantly stepped back into the hall. He seized the door, and, with a loud bang, closed it to between himself and the Chouans. Then, with lightning rapidity, he pushed the heavy bolt home.

The report of a pistol rang out. It came from inside the room. The Man in Grey was leaning his full weight against the door, wondering whether Lefèvre and his men would come to his assistance before the trapped Chouans had time to burst the panels.

He heard Lefèvre's call outside and the heavy tramp of the men. A few seconds of agonising suspense, whilst he literally felt the massive door heaving behind him under the furious onslaught of the imprisoned Chouans, and the commissary with the men of the police burst into the hall. The door fell in with a terrific crash.

The Chouans, caught like foxes run to earth, offered a desperate resistance. But the odds were too great; after a grim struggle across the threshold, which lasted close on ten minutes and left several men of the police bleeding or dead upon the floor, the gang was captured, securely bound and locked in one of the cellars underneath the house, where they were left in charge of half a dozen men until such time as they could be conveyed to Alençon and thence to Bicêtre to await their trial.

VI

It has been impossible, owing to the maze of records, to disentangle the subsequent history of three of these Chouans. The Spaniard, however, was, we know, kept in prison for over five years until, after the Restoration, her friends succeeded in laying her petition of release before the King and she was granted a free pardon and a small pension from the privy purse, "in consideration of the services she had rendered to His Majesty and the martyrdom she had suffered in his cause." On the official list of pensioners in the year 1816 her name appears as "Caroline Mercier, commonly called the Spaniard."

But at Chéron's farm, when all was still, the men of the police gone and the prisoners safely under lock and key, the Man in Grey and the commissary returned to the little room which bad been the scene of the Chouans' final stand. A broken chair was lying by the side of the tall, open chimney, wherein the woman with the swarthy skin and jet-black eyes had concealed the stolen treasure. The accredited agent had no difficulty in finding the secret hiding-place; about a foot up the chimney an iron door was let into the solid wall. A little manipulation of his deft fingers soon released the secret spring, and the metal panel glided gently in its grooves.

M. de Kerblay's precious ring and some twenty thousand francs in money gladdened the sight of the worthy commissary of police.

"But how did you guess?" he asked of the Man in Grey, when, half an hour later, the pair were ambling along the road back towards Alençon.

"While you were getting ready for our second expedition, my dear Monsieur Lefèvre," replied the Man in Grey, "I took the simple precaution of ascertaining whether the farmer Chéron had a wife, a father, and two daughters. Your own records at the commissariat furnished me with this information. From them I learned that though he had a wife, he had no father living, and that he had three grown-up sons, long ago started out into the world. After that, everything became very simple."

"I suppose," quoth the commissary ruefully, "that I ought to have found out about the man Chéron and his family before I went off on that fool's errand."

"You ought, above all, to have consulted me," was the Man in Grey's calm reproof.

III. THE MYSTERY OF MARIE VAILLANT

I

AFTER the capture of the Spaniard at Chéron's farm on that dark night, M. Lefèvre realised that when M. le Duc d'Otrante sent down that insignificant-looking little man in the grey coat to help in the hunt after the astute but infamous Chouans, he had acted--as he always did--with foresight and unerring knowledge of human nature and human capacity.

Henceforward M. Lefèvre became the faithful panegyrist and henchman of the Minister's anonymous agent. He haunted the latter's apartments in the Rue de France, he was significantly silent when the Man in Grey was sneered and jeered at in the higher official circles, and, what is more, when M. Leblanc, sous-préfet of Bourg-le-Roi, had such grave misgivings about his children's governess, it was the commissary who advised him to go for counsel and assistance to the mysterious personage who enjoyed the special confidence and favour of M. le Due d'Otrante himself.

M. Leblanc, who had an inordinate belief in his own perspicacity, fought for some time against the suggestion; but, after a while, the mystery which surrounded Mademoiselle Vaillant reached such a bewildering stage, whilst remaining outside the scope of police interference, that he finally decided to take his friend's advice, and, one morning, about the end of November, he presented himself at the lodgings in Alençon occupied by the accredited agent of His Majesty's Minister of Police.

Of a truth M. Leblanc was singularly agitated. His usually correct, official attitude had given place to a kind of febrile excitement which he was at great pains to conceal. He had just left Madame Leblanc in a state of grave anxiety, and he himself, though he would not have owned to it for the world, did not know what to make of the whole affair. But he did not intend that his own agitation should betray him into a loss of dignity in the presence of the little upstart from Paris; so, after the formal greetings, he sat down and plunged into a maze of conversational subjects--books, the theatres, the war, the victories of the Emperor and the rumoured alliance with the Austrian Archduchess--until the Man in Grey's quiet monotone broke in on the flow of his eloquence with a perfectly polite query:

"Has Monsieur le Sous-Préfet, then, honoured me with a visit at this early hour for the purpose of discussing the politics of the day?"

"Partly, my good Monsieur Fernand, partly," replied the sous-préfet airily. "I desired that we should become more closely acquainted--and," he added, as if with an after-thought, "I desired to put before you a small domestic matter which has greatly perturbed Madame Leblanc, and which, I confess, does appear even to me as something of a mystery."

"I am entirely at Monsieur le Sous-Préfet's service," rejoined the Man in Grey without the ghost of a smile.

"Oh! I dare say," continued M. Leblanc in that offhand manner which had become the rule among the officials of the district when dealing with the secret agent, "I dare say that when I think the matter over, I shall be quite able to deal with it myself. At the same time, the facts are certainly mysterious, and I doubt not but that they will interest you, even if they do not come absolutely within the sphere of your province."

This time the Man in Grey offered no remark. He waited for M. le Sous-Préfet to proceed.

"As no doubt you know, Monsieur Fernand," resumed M. Leblanc after a slight pause, "I own a small house and property near Bourg-le-Roi, some eight kilomètres from this city, where my wife and children live all the year round and where I spend as much of my leisure as I can spare from my onerous duties here. The house is called Les Colombiers. It is an old Manor, which belonged to the Comtes de Mamers, a Royalist family who emigrated at the outset of the Revolution and whose properties were sold for the benefit of the State. The Mamers have remained--as perhaps you know--among the irreconcilables. His Majesty the Emperor's clemency did not succeed in luring them away from England, where they have settled; and I, on the other hand, have continued in undisputed possession of a charming domain. The old moated house is of great archæological and historical interest. It stands in the midst of a well-timbered park, is well secluded from the road by several acres of dense coppice, and it is said that, during the religious persecutions instituted by Charles IX at the instigation of his abominable mother, Les Colombiers was often the refuge of Huguenots, and the rallying-point for the followers of the proscribed faith. As I myself," continued M. Leblanc with conscious pride, "belong to an old Huguenot family, you will readily understand, my good Monsieur Fernand, that I feel an additional interest in Les Colombiers."

Pausing for a moment, the, sous-préfet readjusted the set of his neckcloth, crossed one shapely leg over the other and added with an affable air of condescension:

"I trust that I am not trespassing upon your valuable time, my dear friend, by recounting these seemingly irrelevant, but quite necessary details."

"On the contrary, Monsieur le Sous-Préfet," rejoined the Man in Grey quietly, "I am vastly and, I may say, respectfully interested."

Thus encouraged, M. Leblanc boldly continued his narrative.

"My household," he said, "consists, I must tell you, of my wife and myself and my two children--a boy and a girl--Adèle, aged fourteen, and Ernest, just over twelve. I keep a couple of men and two maids indoors, and three or four men in the garden. Finally, there is my children's governess, Marie Vaillant. She came to us last summer warmly recommended by Monseigneur the Constitutional Bishop of Alençon, and it is her conduct which of late has so gravely disquieted Madame Leblanc and myself.

"But you shall judge.

"At first my wife and I had every reason to congratulate ourselves on having secured such a competent, refined and charming woman to preside over the education of our children. Marie Vaillant was gay, pretty and full of spirits. The children loved her, especially Ernest, who set his entire childish affections upon his young and attractive governess. During the summer lessons were done out of doors, and long expeditions were undertaken in the woods, whence Ernest and Adèle would return, hot, tired and happy. They had played at being explorers in virgin forests, so they told their mother.

"It was only when the evenings waxed longer," continued the sous-préfet, in a tone of growing embarrassment, now that he was nearing the climax of his story, "that Mademoiselle Vaillant suddenly changed. She developed a curious proclivity for promiscuous coquetry."

"Coquetry?" broke in the secret agent with a smile.

"Yes! Marie began to flirt--shamelessly, openly, with every man she came across, visitors, shop-keepers, friends and gardeners. She exercised an almost weird fascination over them; one and all would anticipate her slightest wish; in fact, the men about the house and grounds of Les Colombiers appeared to be more her servants than ours. Moreover, she made an absolute fool of our butler, Lavernay--a middle-aged man who ought to have known better. He has not only pursued Mademoiselle Vaillant with his attentions but also with his jealousy, until Madame Leblanc felt that her whole household was becoming the laughing-stock of the neighbourhood."

"And have you or Madame Leblanc done anything in the matter?" asked the Man in Grey, while M. le Sous-Préfet paused to draw breath.

"Oh,yes! Madame spoke to the girl and I trounced Lavernay. Marie was humble and apologetic and Lavernay very contrite. Both promised to be discreet and sensible in future. At the same time I confess that I was not at all reassured. Within a fortnight we heard through the gossip of a busybody that Marie Vaillant was in the habit of stealing out of the house in the evenings, at an hour when respectable people should be in bed, and after five minutes' start she was usually followed on these peregrinations by the butler. There was no doubt about the whole thing: even our sergeant of police had witnessed these clandestine meetings and bad reported the matter to the local commissary.

"There was nothing for it now but to dismiss the flirtatious governess as quickly as possible. I may say that Madame Leblanc, who had been genuinely fond of the girl, acquitted herself of the task with remarkable tact and gentleness. Marie Vaillant, indeed, belied her name when she received the news of her dismissal. She begged and implored my wife's forgiveness, swore by all she could think of that she had only erred from ignorance; she had no thought of doing wrong; she was innocent of anything but the merest flirtation. Fond of breathing the midnight air which was so balmy and sweet in the woods, she had lately got into the habit of strolling out when she could not sleep and sitting for an hour or so dreaming among the trees. She admitted that once or twice she had been followed by Lavernay, had been very angry with him, and bad seriously rebuked him; but it should never, never happen again--she vowed and swore it should not--if only Madame would forgive her and not send her away from Les Colombiers which was like a home to her, and from Ernest and Adèle whom she loved as if they were her brother and sister.

"But Madame Leblanc was inexorable. Perhaps she felt that quite so much ignorance of the ways of the world and the decorum prescribed to every well educated woman was not altogether credible; perhaps she thought that the lady did protest too much. Certain it is that though she went back on her original pronouncement that the girl must leave the house within twenty-four hours, she refused to consider the question of allowing her to remain permanently.

"It was finally agreed that Marie Vaillant should leave Les Colombiers at the end of the month; but that at the slightest transgression or repetition of the old offence she would be dismissed with contumely and turned out of the house at an hour's notice.

"This happened exactly a fortnight ago," went on M. Leblanc, who was at last drawing to the end of what had proved a lengthy soliloquy; "and I may tell you that since then Mademoiselle Vaillant has grown the model of all the proprieties. Sober, demure, well-conducted, she has fulfilled her duties with a conscientiousness which is beyond praise. When those heavy rains set in a week ago, outdoor life at once became impossible. Adèle and Ernest took seriously to their books and Mademoiselle devoted herself to them in a manner which has been absolutely exemplary. She has literally given up her whole time to their welfare, not only--so Madame Leblanc tells me--by helping with their clothes, but she has even taken certain menial tasks upon herself which are altogether outside her province as a governess. She has relieved the servants by attending to the children's bedroom; she had been making their beds and even washing their stockings and pocket handkerchiefs. She asked to be allowed to do these things in order to distract her mind from the sorrow caused by Madame's displeasure.

"Of course, I gave Lavernay a stern scolding; but he swore to me that though he had followed Mademoiselle during her evening walks, he had done it mostly without her knowledge and always without her consent; a fit of his former jealousy had seized him, but she had reprimanded him very severely and forbidden him ever to dog her footsteps again. After that he, too, appeared to turn over a new leaf. It seemed as if his passion for Marie was beginning to burn itself out, and that we could look forward once again to the happy and peaceful days of the summer."

II

M. le Sous-Préfet had talked uninterruptedly for a quarter of an hour; his pompous, somewhat laboured diction and his loud voice had put a severe strain upon him. The Man in Grey had been an ideal listener. With his eyes fixed on M. Leblanc, he had sat almost motionless, not losing a single word of the prolix recital, and even now when the sous-préfet paused--obviously somewhat exhausted--he did not show the slightest sign of flagging interest.

"Now, my good Monsieur Fernand," resumed M. Leblanc, with something of his habitual, condescending manner, "will you tell me if there is anything in what I have just told you--I fear me at great length--that is not perfectly simple and even stereotyped? A young and pretty girl coming into a somewhat old-fashioned and dull household and finding a not altogether commendable pleasure in turning the heads of every susceptible man she meets! Indiscretions follow and the gossips of the neighbourhood are set talking. Admonished by her mistress, the girl is almost broken-hearted; she begs for forgiveness and at once sets to work to re-establish herself in the good graces of her employers. I dare say you are surprised that I should have been at such pains to recount to you a series of commonplace occurrences. But what to an ordinary person would appear in the natural order of things, strikes me as not altogether normal. I mistrust the girl. I do not believe in her contrition, still less in her reformation. Moreover, what worries me, and worries Madame Leblanc still more, is the amazing ascendency which Marie Vaillant exercises over our boy Ernest. She seems to be putting forth her fullest powers of fascination--I own that they are great--to cementing the child's affection for her. For the last few weeks the boy has become strangely nervy, irritable and jealous. He follows Marie wherever she goes, and hangs upon her lips when she speaks. So much so that my wife and I look forward now with dread to the day of parting. When Marie goes I do verily believe that Ernest, who is a very highly-strung child, will fall seriously ill with grief."

Again M. Leblanc paused. A look of genuine alarm had overspread his otherwise vapid face. Clearly he was a man deeply attached to his children and, despite his fatuous officiousness, was not prepared to take any risks where their welfare was concerned. He mopped his face with his handkerchief, and for the first time since the beginning of the interview he threw a look of almost pathetic appeal on the agent of the Minister of Police.

"Otherwise, Monsieur le Sous-Préfet," said the latter, meeting that look of appeal with a quiet smile, "has nothing occurred to justify your mistrust of Mademoiselle Vaillant's good intentions?"

"Nothing at all," replied M. Leblanc with a nervous hesitation which belied his emphatic words, "except a vague sense of uneasiness-

-the unnatural quiet which came so quickly in the wake of the storm of a fortnight ago; and, as I say, the extraordinary pains which the girl has taken to captivate the boy: so much so in fact that, thinking perhaps Marie still entertained hopes of our complete forgiveness and thought of using the child as an intermediary with us to allow her to remain, Madame Leblanc at my suggestion spoke yesterday very firmly to the girl, and told her that whatever happened our determination was irrevocable. We felt that we could trust her no longer and go she must."

"And how did Mademoiselle Vaillant take this final decision?" asked the police agent.

"With extraordinary self-possession. Beyond a humble 'Very well, Madame,' she never spoke a word during the brief interview. But in the evening, long after the children should have been in bed, Anne--my wife's confidential maid--happened to be in the passage outside Mademoiselle's room, the door of which was ajar. She distinctly heard Marie's voice raised in almost passionate supplication: 'Ernest, my darling little Ernest!' she was saying, 'will you always love me as you do now?' And the child answered fervently: 'I will always love you, my darling Marie. I would do anything for you--I would gladly die for you----' and so on--just the sort of exalté nonsense which a highly-strung, irresponsible child would talk. Anne did not hear any more then, but remained on the watch in a dark corner of the passage. Quite half an hour later, if not more, she saw Ernest slipping out of the governess's room clad only in his little nightgown and slippers and going back to his own room. This incident, which Anne reported faithfully to her mistress and to me, has caused my wife such anxiety that I determined to consult someone whom I could trust, and see whether the whole affair struck an impartial mind with the same ominous significance which it bears for me. My choice fell upon you, my dear Monsieur Fernand," concluded the sous-préfet with a return to his former lofty condescension. "I don't like to introduce gossiping neighbours into my private affairs and I know enough about you to be convinced of your absolute discretion, as well as of your undoubted merits."

The Man in Grey accepted M. Leblanc's careless affability with the same unconcern that he had displayed under the latter's somewhat contemptuous patronage. He said nothing for a moment or two, remaining apparently absorbed in his own thoughts. Then he turned to his visitor and in a quiet, professional manner, which nevertheless carried with it an unmistakable air of authority, intimated to him, by rising from his chair, that the interview was now at an end.

"I thank you, Monsieur le Sous-Préfet," he said, "both for the confidence which you have reposed in me, and for your clear exposé of the present situation in your household. For the moment I should advise you to leave all your work in the city, which is not of national importance, and go straight back to Les Colombiers. Madame Leblanc should not be left to face alone any difficulties which may arise. At the same time, should any fresh development occur, I beg that you will either send for me or come to me at once. I place myself entirely at your disposal."

He did not hold out his hand, only stood quietly beside his desk; but there was no mistaking the attitude, or the almost imperceptible inclination of the head. M. Leblanc was dismissed, and he was not accustomed to seeing himself and his affairs set aside so summarily. A sharp retort almost escaped him; but a glance from those enigmatic eyes checked the haughty words upon his lips. He became suddenly and unaccountably embarrassed, seeking for a phrase which would disguise the confusion he felt.

"My good Monsieur Fernand----" he began haltingly.

"My time is valuable, Monsieur le Sous-Préfet," interposed the Man in Grey; "and at Les Colombiers your son's welfare is perhaps even now at stake."

M. Leblanc--awed and subdued despite himself--had no choice but to make as dignified an exit as was possible in the circumstances.

III

It was barely eight o'clock the next morning when M. Leblanc made an excited and noisy irruption into the apartments of the secret agent of the Minister of Police. The Man in Grey had risen betimes; had brewed himself a cup of coffee and partaken of breakfast. The tray stood on a table beside him, and he was at the moment engaged in the perusal of the newest copy of the Moniteur.

At sight of his visitor he quietly folded and put down his paper. M. Leblanc had literally staggered into the room. He wore riding breeches and boots and his clothes were covered with mud; he had ridden hard and fast, and though his face was deathly pale it was covered with perspiration. His lips were quivering and his eyes had a look of horror and fear which almost resembled madness.

The Man in Grey led him, firmly and gently, to a seat. Without a word he went to a cupboard, took out a flask and a mug and forced a few drops of brandy down the sous-préfet's throat. The latter's teeth were chattering and, through his trembling lips, there came a few hoarsely whispered words:

"My son--my child--he has gone--Oh, my God!"

After he had drunk the brandy, he became a little more composed. He lay back in his chair, with eyes closed, and for a moment it seemed as if he had lost consciousness, for his lips were bloodless and his face was the colour of dead ashes. Presently he opened his eyes and rested them on the small grey figure which stood, quietly expectant, before him.

"My son," he murmured more distinctly. "Ernest--he has gone!"

"Try to tell me coherently what has happened," said the Man in Grey in a quiet tone, which had the effect of further soothing M. Leblanc's overstrung nerves.

After a great effort of will the unfortunate man was able to pull himself together. He was half demented with grief, and it was blind, unreasoning instinct that had led him to seek out the one man who might help him in his trouble. With exemplary patience, the police agent dragged from the unfortunate man, bit by bit, a more or less intelligible account of the extraordinary sequence of events which had culminated a few hours ago in such a mysterious and appalling tragedy.

Matters, it seemed, had been brought to a climax through the agency of feminine gossip, and it was Ma'ame Margot, the wife of one of the labourers, who did the washing for the household at Les Colombiers, who precipitated the catastrophe.

Ma'ame Margot had brought the washing home on the previous afternoon and stopped to have a cup of coffee and a chat in the kitchen of the house. In the course of conversation she drew the attention of Anne, Madame Leblanc's maid, to the condition of Monsieur Ernest's underclothes.

"I have done my best with it," she said, "but I told Mademoiselle Vaillant that I was afraid the stains would never come out. She had tried to wash the things herself before she thought of sending them to me. Whoever heard," added the worthy soul indignantly, "of letting a child of Monsieur Ernest's age go running about like that in the wet and the mud? Why, he must have been soaked through to his waist to get his things in that state."

Later Anne spoke to Mme. Leblanc of what the laundrywoman had said. Madame frowned, greatly puzzled. She had positively forbidden the children to go out while the heavy rains lasted. She sent for Ma'ame Margot, who was bold enough to laugh outright when Madame told her that she did not understand about Monsieur Ernest's things being so stained with wet and mud, as the children had not been out since the heavy rains had started.

"Not been out?" ejaculated Ma'ame Margot, quite as puzzled as her lady. "Why! my man, when he was looking after the sick cow the other night, saw Monsieur Ernest out with the governess. It was past midnight then and the rain coming down in torrents, and my man, he says to me----"

"Thank you, Ma'ame Margot," broke in Madame Leblanc, "that will do."

She waited quietly until the laundrywoman was out of the house, then she sent for Mademoiselle Vaillant. This time no prayers, no protestations would avail. The girl must leave the house not later than the following morning. What her object could have been in dragging her young pupil with her on her nocturnal expeditions Madame Leblanc could not of course conjecture; did she take the child with her as a chaperon on her meetings with Lavernay, or what? Well, whatever her motive, the girl was not a fit person to be in charge of young children and go she must, decided Madame definitely.

This occurred late yesterday afternoon. Strangely enough, Marie Vaillant took her dismissal perfectly calmly. She offered neither explanation nor protest. Beyond a humble "Very well, Madame!" she never said a word during this final interview with her employer, who, outraged and offended at the girl's obstinacy and ingratitude, ordered her to pack up her things and leave the house early next morning, when a carriage would be ready to take her and her effects to Alençon.

Early this morning, not two hours ago in fact, Anne had come running into Madame Leblanc's room with a scared white face, saying that Monsieur Ernest was not in his room and was nowhere to be found. He appeared to have slipped on the clothes which he had worn the previous night, as these were missing from their usual place.

Terribly alarmed, M. Leblanc had sent Anne to bring Mademoiselle Vaillant to him immediately; but Anne returned within a couple of minutes with the news that Mademoiselle had also disappeared. The house was scoured from attic to cellar, the gardens were searched, and the outdoor labourers started to drag the moat. Madame Leblanc, beside herself with dread, had collapsed, half fainting, in the hall, where Anne was administering restoratives to her. Monsieur Leblanc had ordered his horse, determined at once to inform the police. He was standing at his dressing-room window, putting on his riding clothes when he saw Marie Vaillant running as fast as ever she could across the garden towards the house. Her dress clung wet and muddy round her legs, her hair was streaming down her back, and she held out her arms in front of her as she ran. Indeed, she looked more mad than sane, and there was such a look of fear and horror in her face and about her whole appearance, that the servants--stupid and scared--stood by gaping like gabies, not attempting to run after her. In a moment M. Leblanc--his mind full of horrible foreboding--had flung out of his dressing-room, determined to intercept the woman and to wring from her an admission of what she had done with the boy.

He ran down the main staircase, as he had seen Marie make straight for the chief entrance hall, but, presumably checked in her wild career, the girl had suddenly turned off after she had crossed the bridge over the moat, and must have dashed into the house by one of the side doors, for at the moment that M. Leblanc reached the hall he could hear her tearing helter-skelter up the uncarpeted service stairs. No one so far had attempted to stop her. M. Leblanc now called loudly to the servants to arrest this mad woman in her flight; there was a general scrimmage, but before anyone could reach the top landing, Marie had darted straight into her employers' bedroom and had locked and bolted the heavy door.

"You may imagine," concluded the unfortunate sous-préfet, who had been at great pains to give his narrative some semblance of coherence, "that I was the first to bang against the bedroom door and to demand admittance of the wretched creature. At first there was no reply, but through the solid panelling we could hear a distinct and steady hammering which seemed to come from the farther end of the room. All the doors in the old house are extraordinarily heavy, but the one that gives on my wife's and my bedroom is of unusually massive oak with enormous locks and bars of iron and huge iron hinges. I felt that it would be futile to try to break it open, and, frankly, I was not a little doubtful as to what the wretched woman might do if brought to bay. The windows of the bedroom as well as those of the dressing-room adjoining give directly on the moat, which at this point is over three mètres deep. Placing two of the men-servants on guard outside the door, with strict orders not to allow the woman to escape, I made my way into the garden and took my stand opposite the bedroom windows. I had the width of the moat between me and the house. The waters lapped the solid grey walls and for the first time since I have lived at Les Colombiers, the thought of the old Manor, with its lurking holes for unfortunate Huguenots, struck my heart with a sense of coldness and gloom. Up above Marie Vaillant had already taken the precaution of fastening the shutters; it was impossible to imagine what she could be doing, locked up in that room, or why she should refuse to come out, unless----"

The stricken father closed his eyes as he hinted at this awful possibility; a shiver went through him.

"A ladder----" suggested the Man in Grey.

"Impossible!" replied M. Leblanc. "The moat on that side is over eight mètres wide. I had thought of that. I thought of everything; I racked my brains. Think of it, sir! My boy Ernest gone, and his whereabouts probably only known to that mad woman up there!"

"Your butler Lavernay?" queried the Man in Grey.

"It was when I realised my helplessness that I suddenly thought of him," replied the sous-préfet; "but no one had seen him. He too had disappeared."

Then suddenly the full force of his misery rushed upon him. He jumped to his feet and seized the police agent by the coat sleeve.

"I entreat you, Monsieur Fernand," he exclaimed in tones of pitiable entreaty, "do not let us waste any more time. We'll call at the commissariat of police first and get Lefèvre to follow hard on our heels with a posse of police. I beg of you to come at once!"

Gently the Man in Grey disengaged his arm from the convulsive grasp of the other. "By your leave," he said, "we will not call in a posse of police just yet. Remember your own fears! Brought to bay, Marie Vaillant, if indeed she has some desperate deed to conceal, might jump into the moat and take the secret of your boy's whereabouts with her to her grave."

"My God, you are right!" moaned the unfortunate man. "What can I do? In Heaven's name tell me what to do."

"For the moment we'll just go quietly to Les Colombiers together. I always keep a horse ready saddled for emergencies at the 'Trois Rois' inn close by. Do you get to horse and accompany me thither."

"But----"

"I pray you, sir, do not argue," broke in the police agent curtly. "Every minute has become precious."

And silently M. Leblanc obeyed. He had a at once grown as tractable as a child. The dominating personality of that little Man in Grey had entire possession of him now, of his will and understanding.

IV

The first part of the cross-country ride was accomplished in silence. M. Leblanc was in a desperate hurry to get on; he pushed his horse along with the eagerness of intense anxiety. For awhile the police agent kept up with him in silence, then suddenly he called a peremptory "Halt!"

"Your horse will give out, Monsieur le Sous-Préfet," he said. "Allow him to walk for awhile. There are two or three questions I must put to you before we arrive at Les Colombiers."

M. Leblanc obeyed and set his horse to a walk. Of a truth he was more worn-out that his steed.

"Firstly, tell me what kind of fireplace you have in your bedroom," said the other abruptly, and with such strange irrelevance that the sous-préfet stared at him.

"Why," he replied submissively, "there is a fine old chimney, as there is in every room in the house."

"You have had a fire in it lately?"

"Oh, every day. The weather has been very cold."

"And what sort of bed do you sleep in?"

"An old-fashioned fourpost bedstead," replied M. Leblanc, more and more puzzled at these extraordinary questions, "which I believe has been in the house for two or three hundred years. It is the only piece of the original furniture left; everything else was sold by Monsieur de Mamers' agent before the State confiscated the house. I don't know why the bedstead was allowed to remain; probably because it is so uncommonly heavy and is also screwed to the floor."

"Thank you. That is interesting," rejoined the police agent drily. "And now, tell me, what is the nearest house to yours that is of similar historical interest?"

"An old sixteenth-century house, you mean?"

"Yes."

"There is none at Bourg-le-Roi. If you remember, the town itself is comparatively modern, and every traveller will tell you that Les Colombiers is the only interesting piece of mediæval architecture in the neighbourhood. Of course, there are the ruins at Saut-de-Biche."

"The ruins at Saut-de-Biche?"

"Yes. In the woods, about half a kilomètre from Les Colombiers. They are supposed to be the remains of the old farmhouse belonging to the Manor; but only two or three walls are left standing. A devastating fire razed the place to the ground some ten years ago; since then the roof has fallen in, and the town council of Bourg-le-Roi has been using some of the stone for building the new town hall. The whole thing is just a mass of débris and charred wood."

While the two men were talking the time had gone by swiftly enough. Alençon was soon left far behind; ahead, close by, lay the coppice which sheltered Les Colombiers. Some twenty minutes later the two men drew rein in the fine old courtyard of the ancient Manor. At a call from M. Leblanc one of his men rushed out of the house to hold the horses and to aid his master to dismount. The Man in Grey was already on his feet

"What news?" he asked of the man.

The latter shrugged his shoulders. There was no change at Les Colombiers. The two labourers were still on sentry guard outside the bedroom door, whilst the indoor servant, with the head gardener, had remained down below by the side of the moat, staring up at the shuttered windows, and revelling in all the horrors which the aspect of the dark waters and of the windows above, behind which no doubt the mad woman was crouching, helped to conjure up before their sluggish minds.

Madame Leblanc was still lying on a couch in the hall, prostrate with grief. No one had caught sight of Marie Vaillant within her stronghold, and there was no sign either of M. Ernest or of the butler Lavernay.

Without protest or opposition on the part of the master of the house, the Man in Grey had taken command of the small army of scared domestics.

"Monsieur le Sous-Préfet," he said, "before I can help you in this matter, I must make a hurried inspection of your domain, I shall require three of your men to come with me. They must come armed with a stout joist, with pickaxes and a few heavy tools. You yourself and your women servants must remain on guard outside the bedroom door. Should Marie Vaillant attempt a sortie, seize her and, above all, see she does not do herself an injury. Your head gardener and indoor man must remain by the moat. I presume they can swim."

"Swim?" queried M. Leblanc vaguely.

"Why, yes! There is still the possibility of the girl trying to drown herself and her secret in the moat." M. Leblanc promised most earnestly that he would obey the police agent's commands to the letter, and the Man in Grey, followed by the three labourers who carried their picks, a bag of tools and a stout joist, started on his way. Swiftly crossing the bridge over, the moat, he strode rapidly across the park and plunged into the coppice. Then only did he ask the men to precede him.

"Take me straight to the ruins at Saut-de-Biche," he said.

The men obeyed, not pausing to reflect what could be the object of this little man in the grey coat in going to look at a pile of broken stone walls, while M. le Sous-Préfet was half demented with anxiety and a mad woman might either set fire to the whole house or do herself some terrible injury. They walked on in silence closely followed by the accredited representative of His Imperial Majesty's Minister of Police.

Within ten minutes the ruined farmhouse came in sight. It stood in the midst of a wide clearing; the woods which stretched all round it were so dense that even in mid-winter they screened it from the road. There was but little of the original structure left; a piece of wall like a tall arm stretching upwards to the skies, another forming an angle, some loose pieces of stone lying about in the midst of a medley of broken and charred wood, cracked tiles and twisted pieces of metal. The whole place had an aspect of unspeakable desolation. All round the ruined walls a forest of brambles, dead gorse and broom had sprung up, rendering access to the house very difficult. For a moment or two the Man in Grey paused, surveying the surroundings with a keen, experienced eye. At a slight distance from him on the right, the gorse and bramble had apparently been hacked away in order to make a passage practicable to human feet. Without hesitation Fernand, ordering the three men to follow him, struck into this narrow track which, as he surmised, led straight to the ruins. He skirted the upstanding wall, until an opening in the midst of the big masses of stone enabled him to reach what was once the interior of the house. Here progress became very difficult; the débris from the fallen roof littered the ground and there was grave danger of a hidden chasm below, where the cellars may have been.

The Man in Grey peered round him anxiously. Presently an exclamation of satisfaction rose to his lips. He called to the men. A few feet away from where he was standing the whole débris seemed to have been lately considerably augmented. Right in the midst of a pile of burned wood, tiles and metal, a large stone was embedded. It had evidently been very recently detached from the high upstanding wall, and had fallen down amidst a shower of the decayed mortar, wet earth, and torn lichen and moss, which littered the place.

In obedience to the commands of the Man in Grey, the labourers took up their picks, and set to work to clear the débris around the fallen stone, the police agent standing dose by, watching them. They had not done more than bury their tools once in the litter of earth and mortar, when their picks encountered something soft.

"Drop your tools," commanded the Man in Grey.

"Your hands will suffice to unearth what lies below." It was the body of a man crushed almost past recognition by the weight of the fallen masonry. The labourers extricated it from the fragments of wood and metal and dragged it into the open.

"By his clothes," said one of the men, in answer to a peremptory query from the Man in Grey, "I guess he must be the butler, François Lavernay."

The secret agent made no comment. Not a line of his pale, colourless face betrayed the emotion he felt--the emotion of the sleuth-hound which knows that it is on the track of its quarry. He ordered the body to be decorously put on one side and took off his own loose mantle to throw over it. Then he bade the men resume their work. They picked up their tools again and tried to clear the rubbish all round the fallen stone.

"We must move that stone from its place," the man in the grey coat had said, and the labourers, impelled by that air of assurance and authority which emanated from the insignificant little figure, set to with a will. Having cleared the débris , they put their shoulders to the stone, helped by the secret agent whose strength appeared out of all proportion to his slender frame. By and by the stone became dislodged and, with another effort, rolled over an its flat side. After that it was easy to move it some three or four feet farther on.

"That will do!" commanded the Man in Grey.

Underneath the stone there now appeared a square flat slab of granite embedded into the soil with cement and concrete. One piece of this slab had seemingly been cut or chiselled away and then removed, displaying a cavity about a foot and a half square. In the centre of the slab was an iron ring to which a rope was attached, the other end being lost within the cavity.

The labourers were staring at their find open-mouthed; but the secret agent was already busy hauling up the rope. The end of it was formed into a loop not large enough to pass over a man's shoulders. "Just as I thought," he muttered between his teeth.

Then he lay down on his stomach and with his head just over the small cavity he shouted a loud "Hallo!" From down below there came no answer save a dull, resounding echo. Again and again the Man in

Grey shouted his loud "Hallo!" into the depths, but, eliciting no reply, at last he struggled to his feet.

"Now then, my men," he said, "I am going to leave you here to work away at this slab. It has got to be removed within an hour."

The men examined the cement which held the heavy stone in its place.

"It will take time," one of them said. "This cement is terribly hard; we shall have to chip every bit of it away."

"You must do your best," said the Man in Grey earnestly. "A human life may depend on your toil. You will have no cause to grumble at the reward when your work is done. For reasons which I cannot explain, I may not bring any strangers to help you. So work away as hard as you can. I will return in about an hour with Monsieur le Sous-Préfet." He waited to see the men swing their picks, then turned on his heel and started to walk back the way he came.

It was nearly two hours before the slab of granite was finally removed from its place. M. le Sous-Préfet was standing by with the Man in Grey when the stone was hoisted up and turned over. It disclosed a large cavity with, at one end of it, a flight of stone steps leading downwards.

"Now then, Monsieur le Sous-Préfet," said the police agent quietly, "will you follow me?" M. Leblanc's face was ghastly in its pallor. The sudden hope held out to him by the Man in Grey had completely unnerved him. "Are you sure----" he murmured.

"That we shall find Monsieur Ernest down there?" broke in the other, as he pointed to the hollow. "Well, Monsieur le Sous-Préfet, I wish I were equally sure of a fortune!"

He had a lighted lantern in his hand and began to descend the stone stairs, closely followed by the sous-préfet. The labourers above were resting after their heavy toil. They could not understand all they had seen, and their slow wits would probably never grasp the full significance of their strange adventure. While in the depths below the Man in Grey, holding M. le Sous-Préfet by the arm and swinging the lantern in front, was exploring the mediæval lurking-holes of the Huguenots, the three labourers were calmly munching their bread and cheese.

V

The searchers found the boy lying unconscious not very far from the stairs. A dark lantern had fallen from his hand and been extinguished. A large heavy box with metal handles stood close behind him; a long trail behind the box showed that the plucky child had dragged it along by its handle for a considerable distance. How he had managed to do so remained a marvel. Love and enthusiasm had lent the puny youngster remarkable strength. The broken-hearted father lifted his unconscious child in his arms. Obviously he had only fainted--probably from fright--and together the little procession now worked its way back into the open.

"Can you carry your boy home, Monsieur le Sous-Préfet," asked the Man in Grey, "while we attend to your unfortunate butler?"

But he had no need to ask. Already M. Leblanc, closely hugging his precious burden, was striding bravely and manfully through the coppice beyond.

The Man in Grey arrived at Les Colombiers a quarter of an hour after the sous-préfet had seen his boy snugly laid in his mother's arms. The child was far too weak and too highly strung to give a clear account of the events which had landed him alone and unconscious inside the disused hiding-place, with his only means of exit cut off. But the first words be spoke after he had returned to consciousness were: "Tell my darling Marie that I did my best."

Afterwards the Man in Grey graphically recounted to the sous-préfet how he came to seek for Ernest beneath the ruins of Saut-de-Biche.

"I followed Marie Vaillant's machinations in my mind," he said, "from the moment that she entered your service. Not a word of your narrative escaped me, remember! Recommended by the Bishop of Alençon, I guessed her to be a Royalist who had been placed in your house for some purpose connected with the Cause. What that purpose was it became my business to learn. It was a case of putting the proverbial two and two together. There was, on the one hand, an old moated Manor, once the refuge of persecuted Huguenots and therefore full of secret comers and hiding-places, and, on the other, an émigré Royalist family who had fled the country, no doubt leaving hidden treasures which they could not take away in their flight. Add to these facts a young girl recommended by the Bishop of Alençon, one of the most inveterate Royalist intriguers in the land, and you have as fine a solution of all that has puzzled you, Monsieur, as you could wish. Marie Vaillant had been sent to your house by the Royalist faction to secure the treasure hidden by the Comte de Mamers in one of the lurking-holes of Les Colombiers.

"With this certainty firmly fixed in my mind, I was soon able to explain her every action. The open-air life in the summer meant that she could not gain access to the hiding-place inside the house and she must seek an entrance outside. This manœuvre suggested to me that the secret place was perhaps a subterranean passage which led from some distant portion of the domain to the house itself. There are a number of such passages in France, of mediæval structure. Often they run under a moat.

"Then came the second phase: Marie Vaillant's coquetry. She either could not find or could not open the hiding-place; she needed a man's help. Lavernay, your butler, appeared susceptible--her choice fell on him. Night after night they stole out together in order to work away at the obstacle which blocked the entrance to the secret passage. Then they were discovered. Marie was threatened with dismissal, even before she had found the hidden treasure. She changed her tactics and inveigled your boy into her service. Why? Because she and Lavernay were too weak and clumsy. They had only succeeded in disclosing one small portion of the entrance to the secret lair; a portion not large enough to allow of the passage of an adult. So your boy was cajoled, endeared, fascinated. Highly strung and nervous, he was ready to dare all for the sake of the girl whom he loved with the ardour of unawakened manhood. He is dragged through the woods and shown the place; he is gradually familiarised with the task which lies before him. Then once more discovery falls on Marie Vaillant like a thunderbolt.

"There is only one more night wherein she can effect her purpose. Can you see them she and Lavernay and your boy--stealing out at dead of night to the ruins; the boy primed in what he has to do, lowered by a cord into the secret passage, dark lantern in hand? Truly the heroism of so young a child passes belief! Lavernay and Marie Vaillant wait above, straining their ears to hear what is going on below. The underground passage, remember, is over half a kilomètre in length. I explored it as far as I could. It goes under the moat and I imagine has its other entrance in your bedroom at Les Colombiers. Ernest had to go some way along it ere he discovered the box which contained the treasure. With truly superhuman strength he seizes the metal handle an drags his burden wearily along. At last he has reached the spot where the cord still dangles from above. He gives the preconcerted signal but receives no reply. Distracted and terror-stricken, he calls again and again until the horror of his position causes him to lose consciousness.

"Above the tragedy is being consummated. Loosened by recent heavy rains, a large piece of masonry comes crashing down, burying in its fall the unfortunate Lavernay and hopelessly blocking the entrance to the secret passage. Picture to yourself Marie Vaillant pitting her feeble strength against the relentless stone, half-crazed with the thought of the child buried alive beneath her feet. An oath to her party binds her to secrecy! She dares not call for help. Almost demented, blind instinct drives her to the one spot whence she might yet be able to render assistance to the child--your bedroom, where I'll wager that either inside the chimney or behind the head of the old-fashioned bedstead you will find the panel which masks the other entrance to the secret passage."

The Man in Grey suspended his story and, guided by his host, triade his way upstairs to the landing outside the bedroom door.

"Call to the poor woman, Monsieur le Sous-Préfet," he commanded. "Tell her that the child is safe and well. Perhaps she will come out of her own accord. It were a pity to break this magnificent door."

Presently Marie Vaillant, summoned by her employer, who assured her repeatedly that Ernest was safe and well, was heard to unlock the door and to draw the bolts. Next moment she stood under the heavy oak lintel, her face as white as a shroud, her eyes staring wildly before her, her gown stained, her hands bleeding. She had bruised herself sorely in a vain endeavour to move the massive bedstead which concealed the secret entrance to the underground passage.

One glance at M. Leblanc's face assured her that all was well with her valiant little helpmeet and that the two men before her were moved more by pity than by Wrath. She broke down completely, but the violent fit of weeping eased her overburdened heart. Soon she became comforted with the kindly assurance that she would be allowed to depart in peace. Even the sous-préfet felt that the wretched girl had suffered enough through the tortuous intrigues of her fanatic loyalty to the cause of her party, whilst the Man in Grey saw to it that in the matter of the death of Lavernay His Majesty's Police were fully satisfied.

IV. THE EMERALDS OF MADEMOISELLE PHILIPPA

I

AT first there was a good deal of talk in the neighbourhood when the de Romaines, returned from England and made their home in the tumbledown Lodge just outside St. Lô. The Lodge, surrounded by a small garden, marked the boundary of the beautiful domain of Torteron, which had been the property of the de Romaines, and their ancestors for many generations. M. le Comte de Romaine had left France with his family at the very outset of the Revolution and, in accordance with the decree of February, 1792, directed against the Emigrants, his estates were confiscated and sold for the benefit of the State. The château of Torteron, being so conveniently situated near the town of St. Lô, was converted into a general hospital, and the farms and agricultural lands were bought up by various local cultivators. Only the little Lodge at the park gates had remained unsold, and when the Emigrés were granted a general amnesty, the de Romaines obtained permission to settle in it. Although it was greatly neglected and dilapidated, it was weatherproof, and by the clemency of the Emperor it was declared to be indisputably their own.

M. le Comte de Romaine, worn out by sorrow and the miseries of exile, had died in England. It was Mme. la Comtesse, now a widow, who came back to Torteron along with M. le Comte Jacques, her son, who had never set foot on his native soil since, as a tiny lad, he had been taken by his parents into exile, and Mademoiselle Mariette, her daughter, who, born in England, had never been in France at all.

People who had known Madame la Comtesse in the past thought her greatly aged, more so in fact than her years warranted. She had gone away in '91 a young and handsome woman well on the right side of thirty, fond of society and show; now, nineteen years later, she reappeared the wreck of her former self. Crippled with rheumatism, for ever wrapped up in shawls, with weak sight and impaired hearing, she at once settled down to a very secluded life at the Lodge, waited on only by her daughter, a silent, stately girl, who filled the duties of maid of all work, companion and nurse to her mother, and her brother.

On the other hand, young M. le Comte de Romaine was a regular "gadabout." Something of a rogue and a ne'er-do-well, he seemed to have no defined occupation, and soon not a café or dancing hall in St. Lô, but had some story to tell of his escapades and merry living.

M. Moulin, the préfet, had received an order from the accredited agent of the Minister of Police to keep an eye on the doings of these returned Emigrants, but until now their conduct had been above suspicion. Mme. la Comtesse and Mlle. Mariette went nowhere except now and again to the church of Notre Dame; they saw no one; and for the nonce the young Comte de Romaine devoted his entire attention to Mademoiselle Philippa, the charming dancer who was delighting the audiences of St. Lô with her inimitable art, and dazzling their eyes with her showy dresses, her magnificent equipage and her diamonds.

The préfet, in his latest report to the secret agent, had jocularly added that the lovely dancer did not appear at all averse from the idea of being styled Mme. la Comtesse one of these days, or of regilding the faded escutcheon of the de Romaines with her plebeian gold.

There certainly was no hint of Chouannerie about the doings of any member of the family, no communication with any of the well-known Chouan leaders, no visits from questionable personages.

Great therefore was the astonishment of M. Moulin when, three days later, he received a summons to present himself at No. 15 Rue Notre Dame, where the agent of His Majesty's Minister of Police had arrived less than an hour ago.

"I am here in strict incognito, my dear Monsieur Moulin," said the Man in Grey as soon as he had greeted the préfet, "and I have brought three of my men with me who m I know I can trust, as I am not satisfied that you are carrying out my orders."

"Your orders, Monsieur--er--Fernand?" queried the préfet blandly.

"Yes! I said my orders," retorted the other quietly. "Did I not bid you keep a strict eye on the doings of the Romaine family?"

"But, Monsieur Fernand----"

"From now onwards my men and I will watch Jacques de Romaine," broke in the secret agent in that even tone of his which admitted of no argument. "But we cannot have our eyes everywhere. I must leave the women to you."

"The old Comtesse only goes to church, and Mademoiselle Mariette goes sometimes to market."

"So much the better for you. Your men will have an easy time."

"But----"

"I pray you do not argue, my good Monsieur Moulin. Mademoiselle Mariette may be out shopping at this very moment."

And when the accredited agent said "I pray you," non-compliance was out of the question.

Later in the day the préfet talked the matter over with M. Cognard, chief commissary of police, who had had similar orders in the matter of the Romaines. The two cronies had had their tempers sorely ruffled by the dictatorial ways of the secret agent, whom they hated with all the venom that indolent natures direct against an energetic one.

"The little busybody," vowed M. Moulin, "sees conspirators in every harmless citizen and interferes in matters which of a truth have nothing whatever to do with him."

II

Then in the very midst of the complacency of these two worthies came the memorable day which, in their opinion, was the most turbulent one they had ever known during their long and otiose careers.

It was the day following the arrival of the secret agent at St. Lô, and he had come to the commissariat that morning for the sole purpose--so M. Cognard averred--of making matters uncomfortable for everybody, when Mademoiselle de Romaine was announced. Mademoiselle had sent in word that she desired to speak with M. le Commissaire immediately, and a minute or two later she entered, looking like a pale ghost in a worn grey gown, and with a cape round her shoulders which was far too thin to keep out the cold on this winter's morning.

M. Cognard, fussy and chivalrous, offered her a chair. She seemed to be in a terrible state of mental agitation and on the verge of tears, which, however, with characteristic pride she held resolutely in cheek.

"I have come, Monsieur le Commissaire," she began in a voice hoarse with emotion, "because my mother--Madame la Comtesse de Romaine--and I are desperately anxious--we don't know--we----"

She was trembling so that she appeared almost unable to speak. M. Cognard, with great kindness and courtesy, poured out a glass of water for her. She drank a little of it, and threw him a grateful look, after which she seemed more tranquil.

"I beg you to compose yourself, Mademoiselle," said the commissaire. "I am entirely at your service."

"It is about my brother, Monsieur le Commissaire," rejoined Mademoiselle more calmly, "Monsieur le Comte Jacques de Romaine. He has disappeared. For three days we have seen and heard nothing of him--and my mother fears--fears----"

Her eyes became dilated with that fear which she dared not put into words. M. Cognard interposed at once, both decisively and sympathetically.

"There is no occasion to fear the worst, Mademoiselle," he said kindly. "Young men often leave home for days without letting their mother and sisters know where they are."

"Ah, but, Monsieur le Commissaire," resumed Mademoiselle, with a pathetic break in her voice, "the circumstances in this case are exceptional. My mother is a great invalid, and though my brother leads rather a gay life he is devoted to her and he always would come home of nights. Sometimes," she continued, as a slight flush rose to her pale cheeks, "Mademoiselle Philippa would drive him home in her barouche from the theatre. This she did on Tuesday night, for I heard the carriage draw up at our door. I saw the lights of the lanthorns; I also heard my brother's voice bidding Mademoiselle good night and the barouche driving off again. I was in bed, for it was long past midnight, and I remember just before I fell asleep again thinking how very quietly my dear brother must have come in, for I had not heard the opening and shutting of the front door, nor his step upon the stairs or in his room. Next morning I saw that his bed had not been slept in, and that he had not come into the house at all--as I had imagined--but had driven off again, no doubt, with Mademoiselle Philippa. But we have not seen him since, and----"

"And--h'm--er--have you communicated with Mademoiselle Philippa?" asked the commissary with some hesitation.

"No, Monsieur," replied Mariette de Romaine gravely. "You are the first stranger whom I have consulted. I thought you would advise me what to do."

"Exactly, exactly!" rejoined M. Cognard, highly gratified at this tribute to his sagacity. "You may rely on me, Mademoiselle, to carry on investigations with the utmost discretion. Perhaps you will furnish me with a few details regarding this--er--regrettable occurrence."

There ensued a lengthy period of questioning and cross-questioning. M. Cognard was impressively official. Mademoiselle de Romaine, obviously wearied, told and retold her simple story with exemplary patience. The Man in Grey, ensconced in a dark corner of the room, took no part in the proceedings; only once did he interpose with an abrupt question:

"Are you quite sure, Mademoiselle," he asked, "that Monsieur le Comte did not come into the house at all before you heard the barouche drive off again?"

Mariette de Romaine gave a visible start. Clearly she had had no idea until then that anyone else was in the room besides herself and the commissary of police, and as the quaint, grey-clad figure emerged suddenly from out the dark corner, her pale cheeks assumed an even more ashen hue. Nevertheless, she replied quite steadily:

"I cannot be sure of that, Monsieur," she said; "for I was in bed and half asleep, but I am sure my brother did not sleep at home that night."

The Man in Grey asked no further questions; he had retired into the dark corner of the room, but--after this little episode--whenever Mariette de Romaine looked in that direction, she encountered those deep-set, colourless eyes of his fixed intently upon her.

After Mademoiselle de Romaine's departure, M. Cognard turned somewhat sheepishly to the Man in Grey.

"It does seem," he said, "that there is something queer about those Romaines, after all."

"Fortunately," retorted the secret agent, "you have complied with my orders, and your men have never once lost sight of Mademoiselle or of Madame her mother."

M. Cognard made no reply. His round face had flushed to the very roots of his hair.

"Had you not better send at once for this dancer--Philippa?" added the Man in Grey.

"Of course--of course----" stammered the commissary, much relieved.

III

Mademoiselle Philippa duly arrived, in the early afternoon, in her barouche drawn by two magnificent English horses. She appeared dressed in the latest Paris fashion and was greeted by M. Cognard with the gallantry due to her beauty and talent.

"You have sent for me, Monsieur le Commissaire?" she asked somewhat tartly, as soon as she had settled herself down in as becoming an attitude as the office chair would allow.

"Oh, Mademoiselle," said the commissary deprecatingly, "I did so with deep regret at having to trouble you."

"Well? And what is it?"

"I only desired to ask you, Mademoiselle, if you have seen the Comte de Romaine recently."

She laughed and shrugged her pretty shoulders.

"The young scamp!" she said lightly. "No, I haven't seen him for two days. Why do you ask?"

"Because the young scamp, as you so pertinently call him, has disappeared, and neither his mother nor his sister knows what has become of him."

"Disappeared?" exclaimed Mademoiselle Philippa. "With my emeralds!"

Her nonchalance and habitual gaiety suddenly left her. She sat bolt upright, her small hands clutching the arms of her chair, her face pale and almost haggard beneath the delicate layer of rouge.

"Your emeralds, Mademoiselle?" queried M. Cognard in dismay.

"My emeralds!" she reiterated with a catch in her voice. "A necklace, tiara and earrings--a gift to me from the Emperor of Russia when I danced before him at St. Petersburg. They are worth the best part of a million francs, Monsieur le Commissaire. Oh! Monsieur de Romaine cannot have disappeared--not like that--and not with my emeralds!" She burst into tears and M. Cognard had much ado to reassure her. Everything would be done, he declared, to trace the young scapegrace. He could not dispose of the emeralds, vowed the commissary, without being apprehended and his booty being taken from him.

"He can dispose of them abroad," declared Mademoiselle Philippa, who would not be consoled. "He may be on the high seas by now--the detestable young rogue."

"But how came Mademoiselle Philippa's priceless emeralds in the hands of that detestable young rogue?" here interjected a quiet, even voice.

Mademoiselle turned upon the Man in Grey like a young tiger-cat that has been teased.

"What's that to you?" she queried.

He smiled.

"Are we not all trying to throw light on a mysterious occurrence?" he asked.

"Monsieur de Romaine wanted to show my emeralds to his mother," rejoined Mademoiselle, somewhat mollified and not a little shamefaced. "I had promised to be his wife--Madame la Comtesse had approved--she looked upon me as a daughter--I had been up to her house to see her--she expressed a wish to see my emeralds--and so on Tuesday I entrusted them to Monsieur de Romaine--and--and----"

Once more her voice broke and she burst into tears. It was a pitiably silly story, of course--that of the clumsy trap set by a fascinating rogue--the trap into which hundreds of thousands of women have fallen since the world began, and into which as many will fall again so long as human nature does not undergo a radical change.

"And when you drove Monsieur de Romaine home on that Tuesday night," continued the Man in Grey; "he had your emeralds in his possession?"

"Yes," replied Mademoiselle through her tears. "He had them in the inside pocket of his coat. I took leave of him at the Lodge. He waved his hand to me and I drove off. That, is the last I have seen of him--the scamp!"

Mademoiselle Philippa was evidently taking it for granted that Jacques de Romaine had stolen her emeralds, and she laughed derisively when M. Cognard suggested that mayhap the unfortunate young man had been waylaid and robbed and afterwards murdered by some malefactor who knew that he had the jewels in his possession.

"Well!" commented the dancer with a shrug of her shoulders, "'tis for you, my good Commissaire, to find either my emeralds for me or the murdered body of Monsieur le Comte de Romaine."

After which parting shot Mademoiselle took her departure, leaving an atmosphere of cosmetics and the lingering echo of the frou-frou of silken skirts.

IV

The commissary accompanied Mademoiselle Philippa to the door. He was not looking forward with unadulterated pleasure to the next half-hour, when of a surety that fussy functionary from Paris would set the municipal authorities by the ears for the sake of an affair which, after all, was not so very uncommon in these days--a handsome rogue, a foolish, trusting woman, valuable jewellery. The whole thing was very simple and the capture of the miscreant a certainty.

"How was he going to dispose of the emeralds," argued M. Cognard to himself, "without getting caught?" As for connecting such a mild affair with any of those daring Chouans, the idea was preposterous.

But when M. Cognard returned to his office, these specious arguments froze upon his lips. The Man in Grey was looking unusually stern and uncompromising.

"Let me have your last reports about Mademoiselle de Romaine," he said peremptorily. "What did she do all day yesterday?"

The commissary, grumbling in his beard, found the necessary papers.

"She only went to church in the morning," he said in an injured tone of voice, "with Madame la Comtesse. It was the feast of St. Andrew----"

"Did either of the women speak to anyone?"

"Not on the way. But the church was very crowded--both ladies went to confession----"

The Man in Grey uttered an impatient exclamation.

"I fear we have lost the emeralds," he said, "but in Heaven's name do not let us lose the rogue. When brought to bay he may give up the booty yet."

"But, Monsieur Fernand----" protested the commissary.

The other waved aside these protestations with a quick gesture of his slender hand.

"I know, I know," he said. "You are not at fault. The rascal has been too clever for us, that is all. But we have not done with him yet. Send over to the Lodge at once," added the secret agent firmly, "men whom you can trust, and order them to apprehend Monsieur le Comte Jacques de Romaine and convey him hither at once."

"To the Lodge?"

"Yes! Mariette de Romaine lied when she said that her brother had not been in the house since Tuesday. He is in the house now. I had only been in St. Lô a few hours, but I had taken up my stand outside the Lodge that night, when I Mademoiselle Philippa's barouche drew up there and Jacques de Romaine stepped out of it. I saw him wave his hand and then turn to go into the house. The next moment the door of the Lodge was opened and he disappeared within it. Since then he has not been outside the house. I was there the whole of that night with one of my men, two others have been on the watch ever since--one in front, the other at the back. The sister or the mother may have passed the emeralds on to a confederate in church yesterday--we don't know.

But this I do know," he concluded emphatically, "that Jacques de Romaine is in the Lodge at this moment unless the devil has spirited him away up the chimney."

"There's no devil that will get the better of my men," retorted the commissary, carried away despite himself by the other's energy and sense of power. "We'll have the rogue here within the hour, Monsieur Fernand, I pledge you the honour of the municipality of St. Lô! And the emeralds, too," he added complacently, "if the robbers have not yet disposed of them."

"That's brave!" rejoined the Man in Grey in a tone of kindly encouragement. "My own men are still on the spot and will lend you a hand. They have at their fingers' ends all that there is to know on the subject of secret burrows and hiding-places. All that you have to remember is that Jacques de Romaine is inside the Lodge and that you must bring him here. Now go and make your arrangements; I will be at the Lodge myself within the hour."

V

It was quite dark when the Minister's agent arrived at the Lodge. M. Cognard met him outside the small garden gate. As soon as he caught sight of the slender, grey-clad figure he ran to meet it as fast as his portliness would allow.

"Nothing!" he said breathlessly.

"How do you mean--nothing?" retorted the secret agent.

"Just what I say," replied the commissaire. "We have searched this tumbledown barrack through and through. The women are there--in charge of my men. They did not protest; they did not hinder us in any way. But I tell you," added M. Cognard, as he mopped his streaming forehead, "there's not a cat or a mouse concealed in that place. We have searched every hole and corner."

"Bah!" said the Man in Grey with a frown. "Some secret hiding-place has escaped you!"

"Ask your own trusted men," retorted the commissaire. "They have worked with ours."

"Have you questioned the women?"

"Yes! They adhere to Mademoiselle's story in every point."

"Do they know that I--a member of His Majesty's secret police force--saw Jacques de Romaine enter this house on Tuesday night, and that I swear he did not leave it the whole of that night; whilst my own men are equally ready to swear that he has not left it since."

"They know that."

"And what is their answer?"

"That we must demand an explanation from the man who was lurking round here in the dark when Jacques de Romaine had priceless jewels in his possession," replied the chief commissary.

The stern features of the Man in Grey relaxed into a smile.

"The rogues are cleverer than I thought," he said simply.

"Rogues?" growled M. Cognard. "I for one do not believe that they are rogues. If Jacques de Romaine entered this house on Tuesday night and has not left it since, where is he now? Answer me that, Monsieur Fernand!"

"Do you think I have murdered him?" retorted the secret agent calmly.

Then he went into the house.

He found Mme. la Comtesse de Romaine entrenched within that barrier of lofty incredulity which she had set up the moment that she heard of the grave suspicion which rested upon her son.

"A Comte de Romaine, Monsieur," she said in her thin, cracked voice in answer to every query put to her by the Man in Grey, "who is also Seigneur de Mazaire and a peer of France, does not steal the jewels of a dancer. If, as that wench asserts, my son had her trinkets that night about his person, then obviously it is for you who were lurking around my house like a thief in the night to give an account of what became of him."

"Your son entered this house last Tuesday night, Madame," answered Fernand firmly, "and has not been out of it since."

"Then I pray you find him, Sir," was Madame de Romaine's rejoinder.

Mademoiselle Mariette's attitude was equally uncompromising. She bore every question and cross-question unflinchingly. But when the secret agent finally left her in peace to initiate a thorough search inside that house which so bafflingly refused to give up its secret, she turned to the chief commissary of police.

"Who is that anonymous creature," she queried with passionate indignation, "who heaps insults and tortures upon my dear mother and me? Why is he not being questioned? Whose is the hidden hand that shields him when retribution should be marking him for its own?"

Whose indeed? The commissary of police was at his wits' end. Even the Man in Grey--resolute, systematic and untiring--failed to discover anything suspicious in the Lodge. It had often been said of him that no secret hiding-place, no secret panel or lurking-hole could escape his eagle eye, and yet, to-day, after three hours' persistent search, he was forced to confess he had been baffled.

Either his men had relaxed their vigilance at some time since that fateful Tuesday night, and had allowed the rogue to escape, or the devil had indeed spirited the young Comte de Romaine up the chimney.

Public opinion at once went dead against the authorities. Mademoiselle de Romaine had taken good care that the story of the man lurking round the Lodge on the night her brother disappeared should be known far and wide. That that man happened to be a mysterious and anonymous member of His Majesty's secret police did not in any way allay the popular feeling. The worthy citizens of St. Lô loudly demanded to know why he was not brought to justice. The préfet, the commissary, the procureur, were all bombarded with correspondence. Indignation meetings were held in every parish of the neighbourhood. Indeed, so tense had the situation become that the chief departmental and municipal officials were tendering their resignations wholesale, for their position, which already was well-nigh intolerable, threatened to become literally dangerous. Sooner or later the public would have to be told that the Man in Grey, on whom so grave a suspicion now rested, had mysteriously vanished, no one knew whither, and that no one dared to interfere with his movements, on pain of having to deal with M. le Duc d'Otrante, His Majesty's Minister of Police, himself.

VI

Towards the end of December Mme. la Comtesse de Romaine announced her intention of going abroad.

"There is no justice in this country," she had declared energetically, "or no power on earth would shield my son's murderer from the gallows."

Of Jacques de Romaine there had been no news, nor yet of the Man in Grey. The procureur impérial, feeling the sting of Madame's indignation, had been over-courteous in the matter of passports, and everything was got ready in view of the de Romaines' departure. Madame had decided to go with Mademoiselle Mariette to Rome, where she had many friends, and the first stage of the long journey had been fixed for the 28th, when the two ladies proposed to travel by private coach as far as Caen, to sleep there, and thus be ready in the early morning for the mail-coach which would take them to Paris.

A start was to be made at midday. In the morning Mademoiselle de Romaine went to High Mass at Notre Dame, it being the feast of the Holy Innocents. The church was very crowded, but Mariette had arrived early, and she had placed her prie-dieu behind the shelter of one of the pillars, where she sat quite quietly, fingering her rosary, while the large congregation filed in. But all the while her thoughts were plainly not at her devotions. Her dark eyes roamed restlessly over every face and form that gathered near her, and there was in her drawn face something of the look of a frightened hare, when it lies low within its form, fearful lest it should be seen.

It was a bitterly cold morning, and Mariette wore a long, full cape, which she kept closely wrapped round her shoulders. Anon a verger came round with foot-warmers which he distributed, in exchange for a few coppers, to those who asked for them. One of these he brought to Mariette and placed it under her feet. As he did so an imperceptible look of understanding passed from her to him. Then the priests followed in, the choir intoned the Introit, the smoke of incense rose to the exquisitely carved roof, and everyone became absorbed in prayer.

Mariette de Romaine, ensconced behind the pillar, sat still, until, during the Confiteor, when all heads were buried between clasped hands, she stooped and apparently rearranged the position of her foot-warmer. Anyone who had been closely watching her would have thought that she had lifted it from the ground and was hugging it tightly under her cloak. No doubt her hands were cold.

Just before the Elevation a man dressed in a rough workman's blouse, his bare feet thrust into shabby shoes of soft leather, came and knelt beside her. She tried to edge away from him, but the pillar was in the way and she could not retreat any farther. Then suddenly she caught the man's glance, and he--very slowly--put his grimy hand up to the collar of his blouse and, just for an instant, turned it back: on the reverse side of the collar was sewn a piece of white ribbon with a fleur-de-lys roughly embroidered upon it--the device of the exiled Bourbon princes. A look of understanding, immediately followed by one of anxious inquiry, spread over Mariette de Romaine's face, but the man put a finger to his lips and gave her a scarcely perceptible reassuring nod.

After the conclusion of the service and during the usual noise and bustle of the departing congregation the man drew a little nearer to Mariette and whispered hurriedly:

"Do not go yet--there are police spies outside."

Mariette de Romaine was brave, at times even reckless, but at this warning her pale cheeks became almost livid. She hugged the bulky thing which she held under her cloak almost convulsively to her breast.

"What am I to do?" she whispered in response.

"Wait here quietly," rejoined the man, "till the people have left. I can take you through the belfry and out by a postern gate I know of."

"But," she gasped hoarsely, for her throat felt dry and parched, "afterwards?"

"You can come to my lodgings," he replied. "We'll let Madame know--and then we shall have to think what best to do."

"Can you find White-Beak?" she asked.

"What for?"

"I could give him the----"

"Hush!" he broke in quickly.

"I should like Monsieur le Chanoine to keep them again; we shall have to make fresh arrangements----"

"Hush!" he reiterated more peremptorily. "We can do nothing for the moment except arrange for your safety."

The man spoke with such calm and authority that instinctively Mariette felt reassured. The bustle round them, people coming and going, chairs creaking against the flagstones, had effectually drowned the whispered colloquy. Now the crowd was thinning: the man caught hold of Mariette's cloak, and she, obediently, allowed him to lead her. He seemed to know his way about the sacred edifice perfectly, and presently, after they had crossed the belfry and gone along a flagged corridor, he opened a low door, and she found herself in the open in the narrow passage behind the east end of the church. Her guide was supporting her by the elbow and she, still hugging her precious burden, walked beside him without further question. He led her to a house in a street close by, where he appeared to be at home. After climbing three flights of steps, he knocked vigorously at a door which was immediately opened by a man also dressed in a rough blouse, and ushered Mariette de Romaine into an apartment of the type usually inhabited by well-to-do artisans. After crossing a narrow hall she entered a sitting-room wherein the first sight that greeted her tired eyes was a bunch of roughly fashioned artificial white lilies in the centre of a large round table. Fully reassured, though thoroughly worn out with the excitement of the past few minutes, the girl sank into a chair and threw open the fastening of her cloak. The bulky parcel, cleverly contrived to look like a foot-warmer, lay upon her lap.

"Now we must let Madame la Comtesse know," said the man who had been her guide, in a quiet, matter-of-fact tone. "Oh, it will be quite safe," he added, seeing a look of terror had spread over Mariette de Romaine's face. "I have a comrade here, Hare's-Foot--you know him, Mademoiselle?"

She shook her head.

"He is well known in St. Lô," continued the man simply. "Supposed to be harmless. His real name is Pierre Legrand. The police spies have never suspected him--the fools. But he is one of us--and as intrepid as he is cunning. So if you will write a few words, Mademoiselle, Hare's-Foot will take them at once to Madame la Comtesse."

"What shall I say?" asked Mariette, as she took up pen and paper which her unknown friend was placing before her.

"Only that you became faint in church," he suggested, "and are at a friend's house. Then request that Madame la Comtesse should come to you at once: the bearer of your note will guide her."

Obediently the girl wrote as he advised, the man watching her the while. Had Mariette de Romaine looked up she might have seen a strange look in his face--a look that was almost of pity.

The letter was duly signed and sealed and handed over to Hare's-Foot--the man who had opened the door of the apartment--and he at once went away with it.

After that perfect quietude reigned in the small room. Mariette leaned her head against the back of her chair. She felt very tired.

"Let me relieve you of this," said her companion quietly, and without waiting for her acquiescence he took the bulky parcel from her and put it on the table. Then Mariette de Romaine fell into a light sleep.

VII

She was aroused by the sound of her mother's voice. Madame la Comtesse de Romaine was in her turn being ushered into the apartment, and was already being put in possession of the facts connected with her daughter's letter which had summoned her hither.

"I guessed at once that something of the sort had happened," was Madame's dry and unperturbed comment. "Mariette was not likely to faint while she had those emeralds in her charge. You, my men," she added, turning to her two interlocutors, "have done well by us. I don't yet know how you came to render us and our King's cause this signal service, but you may be sure that it will not go unrewarded. His Majesty himself shall hear of it--on the faith of a de Romaine."

"And now, Madame la Comtesse," rejoined the man in the rough blouse quietly, "I would suggest that Mademoiselle and yourself don a suitable disguise, while Hare's-Foot and I arrange for a safe conveyance to take you out of St. Lô at once. We have most effectually given the police spies the slip, and while they are still searching the city for you you will be half way on the road to Caen, and there is no reason why the original plans for your journey to Rome should be in any way modified."

"Perfect! Perfect!" exclaimed Madame enthusiastically. "You are a jewel, my friend."

There was nothing of the senile invalid about her now. She had cast off her shawl and her bonnet, and with them the lank, white wig which concealed her own dark hair. The man in the rough blouse smiled as he looked on her.

"My mate and I have a number of excellent disguises in this wardrobe here, Madame la Comtesse," he said, as he pointed to a large piece of furniture which stood in a corner of the room, "and all are at your service. I would suggest a peasant's dress for Mademoiselle, and," he added significantly, "a man's attire for Madame, since she is so very much at home in it."

"You are right, my man," rejoined Madame lightly. "I was perfectly at home in my son's breeches, and I shall never cease to regret that Jacques de Romaine must remain now as he is--vanished or dead--for as long as I live."

The two men then took their leave, and the ladies proceeded to select suitable disguises. Silently and methodically they proceeded in their task, Mariette de Romaine making herself look as like a labourer's wench as she could, whilst Mme. la Comtesse slipped into a rough suit of coat and breeches with the case born of constant habit. Her short dark hair she tied into a knot at the nape of her neck and placed a shabby three-cornered hat jauntily upon it. Her broad, unfeminine figure, her somewhat hard-marked features and firm mouth and chin made her look a handsome and dashing cavalier.

When a few moments later the sound of voices in the hall proclaimed the return of the men, Mme. la Comtesse was standing expectant and triumphant facing the door, ready for adventure as she had always been, a light of daring and of recklessness in her eyes, love of intrigue and of tortuous paths, of dark conspiracies and even of unavowable crimes glowing in her heart--all for the sake of a King whom

France with one voice had ejected from her shores, and a régime which the whole of, France abhorred.

The door was opened: a woman's cry of joy and astonishment rang out.

"Why Jacques, you young scamp!" exclaimed Mademoiselle Philippa who, dressed in a brilliant dart green silk, with feathered hat and well-rouged cheeks was standing under the lintel of the narrow door like a being from another world. "Where have you been hiding all this while?"

But her cry of mingled pleasure and petulance had already been followed by a double cry of terror. Mme. la Comtesse, white now to the lips, had fallen back against the table, to which she clung, whilst Mariette de Romaine, wide-eyed like a tracked beast at bay, was gazing in horror straight before her, where, behind Philippa's flaring skirts, appeared the stern, colourless face of a small man in a grey coat.

"It was for the mean spies of that Corsican upstart," she exclaimed with passionate indignation, "to have devised such an abominable trick."

Already the Man in Grey had entered the room. Behind him, in the dark, narrow hall, could be seen the vague silhouettes of three or four men in plain clothes.

"Trick for trick, Mademoiselle, and disguise for disguise," said the secret agent quietly. "I prefer mine to the one which deceived and defrauded Mademoiselle Philippa here of close on a million francs' worth of jewels."

"A trick?" exclaimed the dancer, who was looking the picture of utter confusion and bewilderment.

"My jewels?--I don't understand----"

"Madame la Comtesse de Romaine, otherwise Jacques, your fiancé and admirer, Mademoiselle, has time to explain. The private coach which will convey her to Rennes will not be here for half an hour. In the meanwhile," he added, as he took up the parcel of jewels which still lay upon the table, "you will find these at the commissariat of police whenever you care to call for them. Monsieur Cognard will have the privilege of returning them to you."

But Mademoiselle Philippa was far too much upset to wait for explanations. At the invitation of the Minister's accredited agent, she had followed him hither, for he had told her that she would see Jacques de Romaine once more. The disappointment and mingled horror and excitement when she realised what an amazing trick had been played upon her literally swept her off her nimble feet. It was a month or more before she was well enough to fulfill her outstanding engagements.

The de Romaines--mother and daughter--offered no resistance. Indeed, resistance would have been futile, and theirs was not the temperament to allow of hysterics or undignified protestations. Every courtesy was shown to them on their way to Rennes, where they were tried and condemned to five years' imprisonment. But twelve months later the Imperial clemency was exercised in their favour, and they were released; after the Restoration they were handsomely rewarded for their zeal in the service of the King.

The Comte Jacques de Romaine who, as a little lad, had been taken over to England, never came to France till after Waterloo had been fought and won. At the time that his mother impersonated him so daringly and with such sinister results, he was serving in the Prussian Army. Mariette de Romaine subsequently married the Vicomte de Saint-Vaast. She and her husband emigrated with Charles X in 1830, and their son married an Englishwoman, and died in a house at Hampstead in the early 'seventies.

V. THE BOURBON PRINCE

I

"I DON'T see how I can be of any assistance to you, my good Monsieur Moulin. I quite agree with you that it would be a real calamity if a member of the ex-Royal family were to effect a landing in our province, but----" And Monseigneur the Constitutional Bishop of Alençon shrugged his shoulders in token of his inability to deal with the matter.

He was sitting in a small room of his splendid private château, which was situated near Granville. Through the tall window on his left, the magnificent panorama of the rugged coast of Normandy and of the turbulent English Channel beyond was displayed in its limitless glory. The point of Carolles still gleamed beneath the last rays of the cold, wintry sun, but the jagged Dog's Tooth rocks were already wrapped in twilight gloom.

"And it is for our People themselves to realise," continued Monseigneur, with his slow, somewhat pompous delivery, "how much happier they would he if they discarded for ever their misguided allegiance to those degenerate Bourbons, and became law-abiding citizens like the rest of France."

"They'll have no chance to do that," growled the Préfet moodily, "once we get one of those Bourbons sowing rebellion and discontent all over the place. The landing of the Comte d'Artois must be prevented at all costs or we shall have the devil to pay. Those Chouans have been difficult enough to deal with, God knows, but hitherto their want of organisation, their lack of responsible leadership and of coordination have been our salvation. With the Comte d'Artois at their head, and a deal of fictitious enthusiasm aroused by him for the exiled Royal family over the water, we shall have bloodshed, misery, and civil war rife again in this corner of France."

"Monsieur le Ministre," rejoined Monseigneur blandly, "has plenty of spies here. Surely, even if the Comte d'Artois effect a landing, he cannot escape capture at the hands of your well-organised police. His death inside your circuit, my dear préfet, would be a fine feather in your cap."

"Oh, we don't want another martyred Bourbon just yet!" retorted the préfet gruffly. "He'd better die in England, or on the high seas rather than in this part of Normandy. We should be accused of murdering him."

M. le préfet was distinctly perturbed and irritable. A denunciation from some anonymous quarter had reached him that morning: a number of rough fellows--marauding Chouans--had, it appeared, halted at a wayside inn somewhere on the Caen road, and openly boasted that M. le Comte d'Artois, own brother to His Majesty the King, was about to land on the shores of France, and that a numerous and enthusiastic army was already prepared to rally round his flag, and to sweep the upstart Emperor from his throne, and all the myrmidons of the mushroom Empire from their comfortable seats.

The Bishop had listened to the story of the anonymous denunciation and to the préfet's wails of woe most benignly and untiringly for close upon an hour. But he was at last showing signs of growing impatience.

"I think, my dear Monsieur Moulin," he said with some acerbity, "you must yourself admit that this affair in no way concerns me. Granville is not even my official residence. I came here for a much-needed rest and, though my support and advice are always at your disposal, I really must leave you and the chief commissary of police to deal with these Chouans as best you can, and with any Bourbon prince who thinks of paying France an unwelcome visit."

He put up his delicate, beringed hand to his mouth, politely smothering a yawn. He appeared absent and thoughtful all of a sudden, bored no doubt by the fussy man's volubility. He was gazing out of the window, seemingly in rapt contemplation of the beautiful picture before him--the setting sun over the Channel, the gorgeous coast scenery, the glowing splendour of the winter twilight.

The préfet felt that he was dismissed. Respect for Monseigneur warred with his latent irritability.

"I won't intrude any longer," he said ruefully, as he prepared to go.

The Bishop, much relieved, became at once more affable.

"I wish I could he of service to you," he said benignly; "but from what I hear you have a very able man at your elbow in the newly accredited agent of His Majesty's Minister. The préfet of Alençon has spoken very highly about him to me, and--though he was unsuccessful in the matter of the burglary in my Palace at Alençon last October, I believe he has rendered very able assistance to the chief commissary of police in bringing some of those redoubtable Chouans to justice."

"He may have done that" quoth the préfet drily, "but I have not much faith in the little grey fellow myself. The problem confronting us here is a deeper one than he can tackle."

A few minutes later the préfet had finally bowed himself out of Monseigneur's presence.

The Bishop remained seated at his desk, absorbed and almost motionless, for some time after his visitor had departed. He appeared to he still wrapped up in the contemplation of the sunset. The hurried footsteps of the préfet resounded on the great flagged hill below; there had been the usual commotion attendant on the departure of a guest: lackeys opening and closing the entrance doors, a call for Monsieur le Préfet's horse, the clatter of hoofs upon the stone-paved courtyard, then nothing more.

The dignified quietude of a well-ordered, richly appointed household again reigned in the sumptuous château. After a while, as the shades of evening drew in, a footman entered with a lighted lamp, which he set upon the table. But still Monseigneur waited, until through the tall window by his side there appeared nothing but an impenetrable veil of blackness. Then he rose, carefully re-adjusted the crimson shade over the lamp and threw a couple of logs upon the cheerful fire. He went up to the window and opened it and, stepping out on to the terrace, peered intently into the night.

The north-westerly wind was soughing through the trees of the park, and not half a kilomètre away the breakers were roaring against the Dog's Tooth rocks; but, even through these manifold sounds, Monseigneur's keen ear had detected a soft and furtive footfall upon the terrace steps. The next moment a man emerged out of the gloom. Breathless and panting, he ran rapidly across the intervening forecourt and, almost colliding with the Bishop, staggered and fell forward into the room.

Monseigneur received him in his arms, and with a swiftly murmured, "Thank God!" led him to a chair beside the hearth. Then he closed the window, drew the heavy damask curtains closely together and finally came up to the newcomer who, shivering with cold and terror, wet to the skin and scant of breath, was stooping to the fire, trying to infuse warmth into his numbed fingers.

"Someone is on my track," were the first words which fell from his quivering lips.

He was a man verging on middle age, short and stout of build, with a white, flabby skin and prominent, weak-looking eyes. been torn his clothes had almost off his back by the frolic of the gale; he was hatless, and his hair, matted and dank, clung to his moist forehead.

The Bishop had remained standing before him in an attitude of profound respect. "Will your Highness deign to come up to my room?" he said. "Dry clothes and a warm bath have been prepared."

"I'll go in a moment," replied His Highness. He had still some difficulty in recovering his breath, and spoke irritably like a wayward sick child. "But let me tell you at once that our movements have been watched from the moment that we set foot on these shores. The crossing was very rough. The gale is raging furiously. The skipper has put into Avranches. He put me off at the Goat's Creek and left me there with de Verthamont and du Roy. As soon as we started to come hither we realised that there was someone on our track. We consulted together and decided that it would be best to separate. De Verthamont went one way and du Roy another, and I ran all the way here."

"Was your Highness shadowed after that?" asked the Bishop.

"I think not. I heard no one. But then the wind kept up an incessant din."

"And did Sébastien meet your Highness?"

"Yes! In the Devil's Bowl. He followed me at a distance as far as your gates. He thought that he, too, had been shadowed all day. Early this morning he reconnoitred as far as Coutances, and there he heard that a couple of regiments of cavalry and a battery of artillery had arrived from St. Lô."

The Bishop made no further comment. His enthusiasm and excitement of a moment ago appeared to have fallen away from him; his finely chiselled face had become serene and pale; only in his deep-set eyes there seemed to smoulder a dull fire, as if with the prescience of impending doom.

A moment or two later he persuaded the Comte d'Artois to come up to his own private apartments. Here a warm bath, dry clothes and a well-cooked supper restored to the unfortunate Prince a certain measure of courage.

"What's to be done?" he asked with a querulous tone in his hoarse voice.

"For the moment," replied the Bishop earnestly, "I would respectfully beg of your Highness to remain in these apartments, which have the infinite advantage of a secret hiding-place which no police agent will ever discover."

"A hiding-place?" muttered the Prince petulantly.

"I loathe the very idea of lurking behind dusty panels like a sick fox."

The Bishop did not venture on a reply. He went up to the fine mantelpiece at the opposite end of the room, and his hand wandered over the elaborate carving which adorned the high wainscoting. He pressed with one finger on a portion of the carving, and at once some of the woodwork moved silently upon unseen hinges, and disclosed a cavity large enough for a man to pass through.

"It would only be an hour or so at a time, your Highness," he said with respectful apology; "in case a posse of Police makes a descent upon the house."

He explained to his august visitor the mechanism of the secret panel. M. le Comte d'Artois, weary after a long sea journey, fretful and irritable, kept up a constant stream of mutterings sotto voce:

"You and the party wished me to come. I never thought that it would be safe, and if I have to remain in hiding in this rat hole, I might just as well be sitting comfortably in England."

Monseigneur, however, never departed for a moment from his attitude of almost reverential deference. With his own hands he ministered to even bodily comfort of the exalted personage who had found refuge under his roof and only left him when he saw the prince comfortably stretched out upon the bed, and was fully assured that he understood the working of the secret panel.

Then after a deep obeisance he finally bowed himself out of the room. Slowly he descended the dimly lighted stairs which led to his study on the floor below. The pallor of his face appeared more marked than before. A vague feeling of anxiety, not unmixed with disappointment, caused a deep frown to settle between his brows.

The situation, though tense always, had become well-nigh desperate now. With M. le Comte d'Artois under his roof and his movements known to a spy of the Imperial police, every hour, every minute had become fraught with deadly danger, not only to him but to every one of his adherents.

Hundreds of men and women around the neighbourhood at this hour were preparing to meet the Prince--the brother of their uncrowned King--for whose sake they were willing to risk their lives. One false move, one act of cowardice or carelessness, and the death of a Bourbon prince would once more sully the honour of France, whilst countless adherents of the Royal cause would again fall victims to their hot-headed loyalty.

And as the Bishop re-entered his study he gave a short bitter sigh, for memory had swiftly conjured up the vision of that unheroic figure which slept contentedly in the room above, and on whose energy and courage depended the lives of those who still believed in him, and who saw in him only the ideal of a monarchy, the traditions of old France and of the glorious days that were gone.

II

Monseigneur, on entering the study, saw a man standing there waiting for him.

"Sébastien!" he exclaimed eagerly.

The man had the bearing and appearance of a good-class domestic servant--one of those who enjoy many privileges as well as the confidence of their employer. But to a keen psychologist it would soon become obvious that the sombre, well-cut clothes and stiff, conventional demeanour cloaked a more vigorous and more individual personality. The face appeared rugged even beneath the solid mask, and the eyes had a keen, searching, at times furtive expression in them. They were the eyes of a man accustomed to feel danger dogging, his footsteps, to hold his life in his own hands and to take risks which would make the pusillanimous quake.

"How long have you been here?" asked the Bishop quickly.

"Half an hour, Monseigneur. I did not dare follow His Highness too closely. The town and its neighbourhood are bristling with spies. I have had the greatest difficulty throughout the day in giving at least two prowlers the slip and drawing them off His Highness's tracks."

Monseigneur uttered an exclamation of horror.

"I thought I had one at my heels a moment ago," continued Sébastien; "just inside the gates. Someone, I felt, was dogging my footsteps. I fired a random shot into the night, and as luck would have it, I brought down my man."

"Brought down your man?" exclaimed Monseigneur eagerly. "Then----"

"Unfortunately it was not a police spy whom I shot," said Sébastien carelessly, "but Grand-Cerf, one of your keepers."

Monseigneur uttered a cry of horror.

"Grand-Cerf! I had posted him just inside the gates to watch for possible prowlers."

"I didn't know that, and I shot him," repeated Sébastien grimly.

"You killed him?"

Sébastien nodded. The matter did not appear to him to have any importance.

"Now if it had been that accursed spy----" he murmured. Then he added more earnestly: "You will have a posse of police over from Granville to-morrow, Monseigneur--they'll search this house. Somehow or other someone has got wind of the affair--I'd stake my life on it."

"Let them come," retorted the Bishop shortly. "Monsieur le Comte d'Artois will be safe behind the secret panel."

Sébastien shrugged his shoulders.

"For half an hour, yes! But if, as I believe, it is that confounded grey chap from Paris who has shadowed us, then no hiding-place or secret panel will screen us from his prying eyes. It is he who tracked down the Spaniard last November, who laid Monsieur de Saint-Tropèze low, who thwarted Mademoiselle Vaillant. Oh!" added the old Chouan, "if I only had him here between my hands----"

His powerful fingers twitched convulsively. Monseigneur shrugged his shoulders.

"That miserable little Man in Grey," he said drily, "has had the luck so far, I own, but it was because his wits were only opposed to brute force. Monsieur de Saint-Tropèze was clumsy, the Spaniard reckless, the girl Vaillant hysterical. Now we have to defend Monsieur le Comte d'Artois himself--but not with our lives, my good Sébastien--'tis our wits which are going to win the day, right under the very nose of the confounded Man in Grey."

III

An hour or two later, in a small dingy room in one of the most squalid portions of the town, the accredited agent of His Imperial Majesty's Minister of Police was hastily demolishing the remnants of a meagre, cold supper. He appeared footsore and cold. M. Moulin, préfet of St. Lô, sat opposite to him at the table. He seemed gravely agitated and anxious.

"We have done all we really could, Monsieur Fernand," he said fretfully, "with the material at our command. Monsieur le Duc d'Otrante's spies have been very active, and I don't think that we have any cause to complain of the results."

"Well, let's hear the results," said the Man in Grey curtly.

A sharp retort hovered on the préfet's tongue. He did not like the dictatorial ways of this emissary from Paris, and had it not been for M. le Duc d'Otrante's express orders, the Minister's secret agent would have fared ill at the hands of this hidebound official.

"There has been," he resumed with some bitterness, "great activity among the Chouans that are known to us in this neighbourhood. Our spies have discovered that the Comte d'Artois landed on this coast in the early dawn this morning. Unfortunately, they cannot be everywhere, and up to half an hour ago we had found no trace of him that we can rely on; at the same time we have intercepted a letter----"

"Pshaw!" ejaculated the Man in Grey impatiently, "And did your spies inform you by any chance that three strangers were landed by the brig Delphine in the Goat's Creek at dawn this morning?"

"Our informant did not say," remarked the préfet drily.

"I dare say not," rejoined the Man in Grey. "Nor did he tell you, perhaps, that the three strangers were met at the Devil's Bowl by Sébastien, who is, if I mistake not, confidential valet to the Constitutional Bishop of Alençon."

"That is false!" broke in Monsieur le Préfet emphatically. "The loyalty of Monseigneur is beyond question."

"Perhaps," retorted the other with a grim smile. "At any rate, Sébastien guided the three strangers through intricate passes among the cliffs as far as the Dog's Tooth. Here the party separated: one man went one way, another the other. Sébastien and one of the strangers waited about the cliffs until dusk, then they made their way along as far as the outskirts of Monseigneur's property----"

"I protest!" ejaculated the préfet hotly.

But the Man in Grey put up his slender hand with a commanding gesture.

"One moment, I beg," he said quietly. "The stranger lurked about on the outskirts of the park until it was quite dark, then he slipped in through the gates, with Sébastien close at his heels. The gates were at once drawn to and closed. The stranger disappeared in the night. A few minutes later the report of a musket rang out through the darkness, then the soughing of the gale drowned every other sound."

"Some thief," exclaimed the préfet gruffly, "lurking round the château. No doubt Sébastien suspected him, dogged his footsteps and shot him. It is all as clear as daylight----"

"So clear, indeed," observed the Man in Grey calmly, "that you, Monsieur le Préfet, will at once communicate with the chief commissary of police. I want a squadron of mounted men to surround Monseigneur's château and a vigorous search made both inside and outside the house."

"What! Now?" gasped Monsieur Moulin.

"Yes; now!"

"But it is past ten o'clock!" he protested.

"A better hour could not be found."

"But Monseigneur will look upon this as an insult!" exclaimed the préfet, who was deadly pale with agitation.

"For which we'll apologise if we have wronged him," retorted the secret agent quietly. "Stay!" he added, after a moment's reflection. "I pray you at the same time to tell Monsieur le Commissaire that I shall require a closed barouche, with a strong pair of horses and a mounted guard of half a dozen men, to be ready for me in the stable-yard of Monseigneur's château. Is that understood?"

It was. To have even thought of disobedience would have been madness. The very way in which the Man in Grey uttered his "I pray you" sent a cold shiver down M. Moulin's spine, and he still had in the inner pocket of his coat the letter written in the all-powerful Minister's own hand. In this letter M. le Due d'Otrante gave orders that his agent was to be obeyed--blindly, implicitly, unquestioningly--whatever he might command, whomsoever he might bid to execute his orders. One look in that pale, colourless face sufficed to show that he knew the power which had been placed in his hands and would use it to punish those who strove to defy his might.

IV

M. Fantin, commissary of police of Granville, was preparing to execute the agent's orders as transmitted by the préfet. The whole matter was unutterably distasteful to him. Monseigneur the Constitutional Bishop of Alençon was a prelate of such high integrity and proven loyalty, that to put such an insult upon him was, in the opinion of the commissary, nothing short of an outrage. He was pacing up and down the uncarpeted floor of his office in a state of great agitation. In a corner of the room, beside the small iron stove, sat the secret agent of His Majesty's Minister. Calm, unperturbed by the mutterings of the commissary, he only exhibited a slight sign of impatience when he glanced at the clock and noted the rapid flight of time. The squadron of mounted police requisitioned by him was making ready to get to horse. It was then close on eleven o'clock.

A moment later one of the police sergeants entered the office with the news that a mounted courier had just arrived from the château, with a message from Monseigneur to the commissary of police.

"I'll see him at once," said the latter, half hoping that this fresh incident would even now prevent the abominable insult to the Bishop.

"What is it, Gustave?" he asked, for he knew the man as one of the grooms in Monseigneur's service. "An attempt at impudent robbery, Monsieur le Commissaire," replied the man, "which has resulted in a man's death. Monseigneur has sent me over to notify you at once and to ask what he should do in the matter."

M. Fantin threw a look of triumph at the little figure in grey that sat huddled beside the iron stove. The commissary had also advanced the theory of an attempted burglary at the château, and was highly elated to see his deductions justified.

"A robbery?" he exclaimed. "How? When?"

"An hour or two ago, Monsieur le Commissaire," replied Gustave. "Monseigneur will explain. I know nothing of the details except that the rascal overturned a lamp. He was burned to death and nearly set fire to the château. I was sent hither post-haste to see Monsieur le Commissaire----"

"Very good," rejoined the commissary. "Ride straight back to the château and tell Monseigneur that I will be there anon."

As soon as the man had gone, M. Fantin turned complacently to the Man in Grey.

"As you see, my dear Monsieur Fernand," he began, "there is no need to----"

"As your squadron is ready, Monsieur le Commissaire," quoth the agent quietly, "'twere a pity not to give them the exercise. And remember the barouche," he added sharply, "and the mounted guard. Do not on any account leave them behind. My orders are in no way modified."

The commissary swallowed the retort which was hovering on his lips; but he threw a look that was almost vicious at the meagre grey-clad figure.

"Do you accompany us?" he asked with a sneer.

"I will meet you at the château," replied the secret agent simply.

Half an hour later Monseigneur was making the commissary of police welcome at the château. He appeared more upset than he cared to admit by the tragedy enacted inside his house. He was not a young man, and his nerves were severely shaken. When his visitors entered, he was sitting in a large armchair beside the fire in his bedroom; he had a glass in his hand, half filled with some sweet-smelling restorative. One of his male servants was in attendance upon him, bathing his master's forehead with vinegar and water.

Preceded by Sébastien and accompanied by the secret agent and two men of the police, M. Fantin there went to view the scene of the tragedy. The two men remained on guard outside the dining-room, where the drama had taken place. The room still presented a disordered appearance; nothing had been touched, Sébastien declared, in view of M. le Commissaire's visit. But the lamp which hung from the ceiling had been lighted, and by its light the whole, extent of what might have been a measureless disaster was revealed to M. Fantin's horrified gaze.

In the centre of the room on the floor, close to, the large dining-table, there lay a shapeless mass, obviously a human body, charred beyond identification. Only the lower part, the heavy cloth breeches, and high leather boots, though badly scorched, were still recognisable. Beside the body, the rich damask table-cloth lay in a burned and tangled heap, where the wretched man had dragged it down in his fall; and a foot or so away was the heavy lamp which had caused the conflagration. It was lying on its side, with bowl, shade and chimney broken, just as it had rolled out of the man's hand. A narrow streak of oil ran from it to the edge of the mantel-kerb. The rich Oriental carpet was burned in several places, and the table itself was severely scorched, while heat and smoke had begun their work of destruction everywhere on the priceless furniture, until water had rendered their work complete.

Sébastien's account of the tragedy was brief and clear. He had had his suspicions aroused during the day by seeing an ill-clad ruffian sneaking around the park gates, and in the evening, feeling anxious, he made a special tour of the château to see that everything was safe. On entering the dining-room he saw a man standing beside the open window, through which he had evidently just made his way. He--Sébastien--at once drew his pistol, and the man turned to fly; but the aim was good and the man appeared to he hit. He gave a snarl like a wild animal, sprang back into the room, apparently with a view to throwing himself upon his assailant, when his strength failed him. With one hand he clutched at the table, but he tottered and fell, dragging with him both the cloth and the table-lamp, which came down with a crash on the top of him, scattering the oil all over his body. His clothing at once caught fire, and Sébastien, realising the danger to the entire house, instantly ran for the buckets of water, which were always kept in the passage for the purpose, and shouted for assistance.

Within a few moments he and another lackey got the fire under, and no great harm was done, save the shock to Monseigneur's nerves, damage to valuable furniture, and the complete obliteration of the felon's identity.

The commissary of police asked Sébastien a few questions for form's sake. He also took some perfunctory notes. He felt irritable and gravely annoyed with the secret agent for having placed him in such an awkward position vis-à-vis of Monseigneur.

"A squadron of police to investigate a common attempt at burglary," he growled savagely, as Sébastien finally showed him out of the room. "We shall be the laughing-stock of the countryside!"

Sébastien laughed.

"'Tis the Chouans who will be pleased, Monsieur le Commissaire," he said. "They have you safely occupied to-night and can go about their nefarious business unmolested, I am thinking."

The Man in Grey was about to follow, but turned for a moment on his heel.

"By the way, my good Sébastien," he said, "at what time did the tragedy take place which you have so graphically described to us?"

For a second or two Sébastien appeared to hesitate.

"Oh," he replied, "somewhere about six or seven o'clock, Monsieur. I couldn't say exactly."

"What made you wait so long, then, before you sent to Monsieur le Commissaire?"

"There was a little confusion in the house, Monsieur will understand. Monseigneur had given orders at once to send a courier over, but the grooms were at their supper, and it took a little time--we meant to send at once--the delay was unintentional."

"I am sure it was," broke in the commissary, who was still within earshot. "And now, Monsieur Fernand," he added, "I pray you excuse me. The hour is getting late, and I must make my apologies to Monseigneur."

"One moment, Monsieur le Commissaire," rejoined the Man in Grey. "Will you not at least question the other servants who came to Monsieur Sébastien's assistance?"

"No one came to my assistance," Sébastien assured him. "The whole affair was over in a moment."

"But when the shot was fired----"

"By the time some of the domestics arrived upon the scene, I had put out the fire. Then I locked the dining-room door. I knew Monsieur le Commissaire would not wish anything touched."

"Quite right!--quite right!" said M. Fantin querulously. "Now, Monsieur Fernand, will you come?"

"One moment, Monsieur le Commissaire," said the secret agent, and suddenly his whole manner changed to one of commanding authority. "There will be plenty of time for excuses presently. For the nonce you will order your captain to make a thorough search of this château and of the grounds around. You will question every one of the domestics; and remember that I shall be about somewhere--probably unseen--but present, nevertheless, to see that the investigation is minute and thorough. Sébastien will remain in the meanwhile in the custody of these two men here, until I have need of him again."

"By Heaven!" protested the commissaire roughly.

"By Heaven!" retorted the Man in Grey loudly, "you'll obey my orders now, Monsieur le Commissaire, or I shall send you straight to Monsieur the Minister to report upon your own misconduct!"

M. Fantin, at the threat and at the manner in which it was uttered, became as white as a sheet. But he obeyed--at once and without another word. Sébastien's rugged face had shown no sign of emotion as, at a curt word from the secret agent, the two men of the Police closed up on either side and marched him into an adjoining room.

The commissary had taken the threat of the Minister's all-powerful agent very much to heart. His men searched the château through and through, just as if it had been the stronghold of some irreconcilable rebel. The secret agent himself appeared and disappeared, while the search was going on, like some grey will-o'-the-wisp--now in one room, now in another, now a passage, now half-way upstairs, just where least expected. The search took over three hours. During that time Monseigneur himself sat in his room in front of the fire, the very picture of silent and offended dignity. He listened--motionless and dignified--to the commissary's profuse apologies, only now and then accepting the ministrations of the lackey who remained with him throughout, bathing his forehead with vinegar, or mixing a fresh glass of orange-flower water. Of the grey-clad figure which flittered unceremoniously in and out of his private apartments, he took no more notice than if he were a fly.

When presently the police actually invaded his own bedroom, Monseigneur's attitude remained one of unapproachable reserve. Even when the agent passed his hands over the wainscoting and presently found the button that worked the secret spring, Monseigneur showed neither interest nor emotion. The hiding-place itself was found to be empty; the Man in Grey walked into it and out again, in a matter-of-fact, impassive manner, as if he were performing a mechanical and useless job. Neither here nor inside the house, nor in the grounds, nor in any other hiding-place was anyone or anything found to impeach Monseigneur's well-known loyalty.

The unfortunate commissary was covered with confusion. He would gladly have strangled the meddlesome official who had placed him in such an awkward position, or even have relieved his feelings by hurling anathema upon him. But the secret agent appeared indifferent both to the wrath of M. Fantin and to the silent disapprobation of the Bishop. When he was satisfied that the search was done, and well done, he took his leave, but not before.

Monseigneur did not vouchsafe him even a look. But he was quite affable with M. le Commissaire, when the latter finally was allowed to depart.

"Have you any further orders, Monsieur Fernand?" queried M. Fantin with bitter sarcasm, when he had bowed his way out of the presence of the outraged prelate.

"Yes," replied the other; "but I will give them to you outside. And stay," he added as the commissary turned on his heel, silent with pent-up rage, "take Sébastien with you and keep him at the commissariat until further orders."

No chronicler could make a faithful record of all that M. Fantin said to himself and to his sergeant even whilst he executed these orders punctually. Fortunately for his feelings on the way home, the Man in Grey did not elect to accompany him. After he had given his final orders he disappeared in the darkness, and M. Fantin was only too thankful to be rid of that unpleasant presence.

V

In and around the château again reigned that perfect silence and orderliness which pertain to an aristocratic household. The squadron of police had long since departed: even the sound of their horses' hoofs, the clang of metal and rattle of swords and muskets had ceased to echo through the night. For a little while longer soft murmurings and stealthy movements were still heard inside the house as the servants went to bed, and, whilst they undressed, indulged in comments and surmises about the curious happenings of the night. Then, even these sounds were stilled. Monseigneur, however, did not go to bed. He had risen from the armchair, and in it he had installed the man who, for several hours had been diligently ministering to him with vinegar and orange-flower water.

"Your Highness is none the worse for the experience, I trust," he said, as he stooped and threw a log or two into the blaze.

"Tired and anxious," replied the Comte d'Artois querulously.

"A night's rest will soon restore your Royal Highness," rejoined the Bishop with deep respect.

"It was a dangerous game to play," continued the prince peevishly. "At any moment one of those men might have suspected."

"It was the only possible game to play, your Royal Highness," rejoined the Bishop earnestly. "The moment those spies were on your track and mine, the search was bound to follow. Think if the police had come here whilst you were in hiding in this room or even behind the secret panel! Nay! 'twas a mercy Sébastien shot Grand-Cerf in mistake for a spy. It enabled us to invent that marvellous comedy which so effectually hoodwinked not only the police but even that astute agent of the Minister himself. And now," added Monseigneur, as a deep sigh of exultation and triumph rose from his breast, "we can work with a free hand. After to-night's work, this house will never again be suspected. We can make it the headquarters of your Highness's staff. It shall be the stepping-stone to your royal brother's reconquered throne."

The words were scarcely out of his mouth when, in an instant, he paused, his whole attitude one of rigid and terror-filled expectancy. Loud and firm footsteps had resounded upon the flagged terrace, though muffled by the heavy damask curtain which hung before the window. A second or two later the footsteps halted, the mullion was struck with something that clanked, and a voice called out loudly and peremptorily:

"Open, in the name of the law!"

The Comte d'Artois had smothered a cry of horror. He clung to his chair with hands that trembled as if with ague, his face became deathly white, and he stared with wild, wide-open eyes in the direction of the window, whence that peremptory call had come. He was in a state of acute physical terror bordering on collapse. Monseigneur, however, had not lost his presence of mind: "Quick, the secret panel!" he said, and already the slender hand was manipulating the hidden spring. The Comte d'Artois tottered to his feet; the next moment there was a terrific crash of broken glass, the damask curtain was roughly torn aside, and the agent stepped into the room.

"Resistance were futile, Monseigneur," he said quietly, for with a rapid movement the Bishop had reached the bell-pull. "I have half a squadron of police outside, and six men at my heels."

He came further into the room, and as he did so he called to two of his men to stand on either side of Monseigneur. Then he turned to Monsieur le Comte d'Artois:

"I have a barouche and a mounted guard ready to convey your Highness to Avranches, where the brig Delphine with her new skipper is at your disposal for an immediate return trip to England. His Majesty the Emperor deprecates revenge and, bloodshed. He might punish, but he prefers to put the culprit out of the way. If Monsieur le Comte d'Artois will offer no resistance, every respect will be shown to his person."

Resistance would, indeed, have been worse than useless. Even Monseigneur replied to his Highness's look of appeal with one of resignation. He picked up a mantle which lay upon the bed and silently put it round the Prince's shoulders, then he took the hand which His Highness held out to him and kissed it fervently. Half a dozen men closed in around the Prince, and the latter walked with a firm step over the threshold of the window, his footsteps and those of his escort soon ceasing to echo through the night.

"You have won, Monsieur," said the Bishop coldly, when he found himself alone with the Man in Grey. "I am in your hands."

"Did I not say, Monseigneur, that His Majesty deprecated revenge?" said the secret agent quietly. "You have an estate in the South, a château finer than this one, so I'm told. You are free to go thither for an indefinite period, for the benefit of your health."

"Exile!" said the Bishop bitterly.

"Do you not deserve worse?" retorted the Man in Grey coldly.

"I nearly outwitted you, though," exclaimed the Bishop.

"Very nearly, I admit. Unfortunately for your clever comedy, I happened to know that your valet Sébastien shot a man just outside your gates early in the afternoon. When he told me the elaborate story of the attempted burglary I knew that he lied, and, with that knowledge, I was able to destroy the whole fabric of your machinations. As you see, I bided my time. And the moment that you, thinking that you were alone with the Comte d'Artois, threw down your mask I was ready to strike. Let me bid you farewell, Monseigneur," he added in conclusion, and, without a touch of irony. "You can have twenty-four hours to prepare for your journey South, and you will remain in your château there awaiting His Majesty's pleasure."

The next moment the Man in Grey was gone, even as the Bishop's parting words struck upon his unheeding ear:

"Awaiting the return of His Majesty Louis XVIII, by the Grace of God, King of France," Monseigneur called out at the top of his voice.

THE END

In the Rue Monge

I

The Professor swung himself round on the high stool on which he was sitting, and blinked tired, watery eyes at his interlocutor.

"You were saying, milor'?" he asked in his shaky, high-pitched voice.

And the other resumed with exemplary patience:

"I was trying to explain to you, my friend, that no one is safe these days, and that at any moment one of those devils on the Committee of Public Safety might set your name down on the list of the suspects. Now, I promised your daughter over in England that my friends and I would look after you; but even without such a promise. . ."

He paused, for obviously the little man was not really listening. He had begun by trying to be attentive, by trying to understand the import of what his friend was saying; but his attention was already wandering and his pale, tired eyes were turned longingly in the direction of his test-tubes, his microscopes and other scientific paraphernalia which littered his table. Now, when his friend ceased speaking, he again tried to appear interested.

"Yes, yes, my daughter!" he murmured vaguely. "Pretty girl, she was. Married that nice man Tessan; a prosperous farmer he was. They were on their honeymoon in England when this awful revolution fell upon us here. Lucky for them! They were never able to return to France."

He continued to ramble on in this vague, inconsequent way; his friend listened to him with undivided attention. They were such a strange contrast, these two: the powerfully-built Englishman, dressed simply but with scrupulous care, a man with finely-moulded hands and lazy, grey eyes that had at times marvellous flashes in them of enthusiasm and command--a leader of men, obviously, a fearless sportsman and daring adventurer--and his learned friend, a man with wizened body and spine prematurely bent, with noble, thoughtful forehead and timid, quivering mouth. A worse-assorted pair could not easily be found. But they were friends, nevertheless. It was a friendship based on mutual respect, even though there was on the one side a strong element of protective affection and on the other a timid, almost child-like trust.

"I would like to go to England with you some day, milor'," the professor went on with a yearning little sigh. "I believe I could do great things in England. I could meet your famous Jenner and show him some of my own experiments in the field of vaccine. These are not altogether to be despised," he added, with a quaint chuckle of self-satisfaction. "And, believe me, my friend, this Revolutionary government is not made up of asses. They have a certain respect for science, especially for the curative sciences; they know that sickness stalks abroad in spite of all their decrees and their talk of a millennium, and they are not likely to molest those of us who work for the better health conditions of the people."

The Englishman said nothing for a moment or two. He regarded his ingenuous little friend with a kindly, gently-mocking glance. At last he said:

"You really believe that, do you, my good Rollin?"

"Yes, yes, I believe it. I had the assurance lately of no less a personage than the great Couthon, Robespierre's bosom friend, that the Committee of Public Safety will never touch me while I carry on such important experiments."

"You could carry them on so much better in England, my friend. The sense of safety would add zest to your work and you would spare your daughter who loves you a cruel anxiety."

"Ah, yes, yes," Rollin murmured in a somewhat querulous tone. "Poor little Marguerite! She was such a pretty girl! But I will come with you, milor'! Be sure that I will come Only, just now--you understand--I have this great work in hand--a work that would even interest the great Jenner. Therefore," he added, with a bashful little smile, "I will even ask you, milor', to excuse me. The light is growing dim, and I ."

The Englishman rose, smothering a half-impatient sigh.

"You want me to go?"

"No, oh no!" the other hastened to add. "Only, the daylight is--"

"More precious in this case than life," the other broke in, with his engaging smile.

He stood up in the narrow, bare room, a giant in height and strength, looking down with that kindly, all-understanding glance of his on this tiny, wizened form of his friend.

"Do you know," he said lightly, "that I could pick you up now and carry you in my waistcoat pocket straight to your daughter's arms?"

For the first time a look of terror crept into the Professor's eyes.

"You would not do that, my friend," he ejaculated fervently; "not until my experiments--"

"Nothing to do with your experiments, my good Rollin," the Englishman replied. He went to the window and stood for a few seconds looking down on the street below. Then he beckoned to the little man, who, compelled somewhat against his will, stepped down from his high stool, very much like a lean, long-legged stork getting off its perch. The Englishman was pointing to a group of men in the street and Rollin obediently looked down, too. The men wore tattered military tunics and ragged breeches. Their bare feet were thrust into shoes stuffed up with straw; they wore the regulation caps adorned with soiled tri-colour cockades. Two or three of them were leaning against the wall of the house opposite, the others stood desultorily about.

"They are always there," the little Professor remarked. "That is because Citoyen Couthon lives next door. He is a great man, is Citoyen Couthon, and these men are, I think, his bodyguard."

"Perhaps," the Englishman remarked drily. "But, anyway, they would search my waistcoat pocket if they saw it bulging with you in it."

He gave a light laugh and then a sigh. Obviously there was nothing more to be said. The old scientist was like a bewildered rabbit, anxious to get back to its burrow. But there was astonishing courage in that feeble body with a quiet philosophy which so gallant a sportsman as Sir Percy Blakeney could not fail to admire.

With a final hasty good-bye he left Professor Rollin to his tubes and retorts, and with a quick, firm step made his way out of the laboratory and then down several flights of stairs to a dark and disused cellar situated in the basement of the house.

The house itself was one of those vast tenements, which for the past century and more had sprung up all over Paris. It had its inevitable square courtyard, with a well in the centre and rows of iron balconies overlooking it from every floor. Hundreds of lodgers in various stages of poverty, mostly abject, dwelt in the tenements. Families of three or four, or sometimes as many as seven, were herded in single rooms. At each of the four angles of the courtyard there was a staircase, dark, dank and unspeakably dirty, since it was no one's business to keep them clean.

It was out of this rabbit warren that, an hour or two later, there stepped into the street an ugly, misshapen creature in ragged shirt and tattered breeches, wearing a knitted cap over a mop of unkempt and mouse-coloured hair. He hobbled along on one leg and a wooden stump, which he banged against the stairs as he came up from the basement where were situated the most squalid of all the apartments, some of them little more than unlit, unventilated cellars.

The group of men whom Professor Rollin had described as Couthon's bodyguard scarcely glance at him. Their attention appeared to be mostly taken up with a window on one of the upper floors, through which could be perceived the wizened figure of Professor Rollin, busy with his test-tubes and microscope.

II

The commissariat of police of the English Section was a low, narrow building sandwiched between a couple of taller houses in the narrow, ill-lit Rue Monge. It was not one of the busy commissariats of the city, because, being situated in so poor and squalid a quarter, there was not a great number of bourgeois and aristocrats to be hauled up before the commissary in the course of the day. True that once or twice proscribed aristos ahd been discovered lurking perdu in one of other of the tenement houses where only the poor congregate but, on the whole, the citizen commissary, by name Bossut, had mostly to deal with malefactors, night birds and suchlike, not bad enough to send to the guillotine, and thus obtain commendation for his zeal, or even promotion such as came in the way of colleagues who were able to make successful hauls of suspects and traitors.

Indeed, the citizen commissary felt distinctly depressed on this evening. He had sent a couple of pilferers to gaol, three young ruffians to the whipping-post and arrested a stupid old man named Rollin, who styled himself professor and spent his time playing about with glass tubes and instruments and all sorts of poisonous concoctions. A harmless fool enough, but Bossut happened to catch a rumour that this Rollin had a daughter married to an emigré--a rich man, seemingly, who had lived all these years in luxury in England, the arch-enemy of France. Now a man who had a son-in-law of that type was clearly a traitor himself and Bossut, in ordering the arrest of the Professor, had vague hopes that something out of the common would come of it--a sensational trial, perhaps, that would bring in its train that commendation from his superiors, or even that promotion which was the dream of the obscure commissary.

But, alas, nothing so far had come of this arrest. Of course, the old fool would be sent to the guillotine--that was a foregone conclusion--but strive as he might, Bossut could not discover anything in the Professor's dossier that would turn his trial into a sensation.

It was hard luck. And now that the lamp was lighted and sent its black, sooty smoke up to the ceiling, without shedding much light into the room, Citizen Bossut felt that there was nothing else to do but to drown his melancholy in a bottle of wine, the best that could be got these hard times. He was just beginning to feel comfortably drowsy, and sat stretched out in a rickety armchair in front of the iron stove, toasting his legs, when his lieutenant, Citizen Grisar, came to announce that a man, who wouldn't give his name, desired to speak with the citizen commissary.

"What does he want?" the latter asked between two prodigious yawns.

"He wouldn't say, citizen," the lieutenant replied.

"Then tell him to go to the devil!"

"Yes, citizen."

Grisar slouched out of the room and the worthy commissary once more tried to compose himself to sleep; but the next moment he was rudely brought to his feet by the sound of loud altercation, much shouting and swearing, and finally by the door of his own sanctum being violently thrown open and a raucous voice shouting hoarsely:

"Ah ça! What kind of a sacré aristo is the citizen commissary, that honest patriots are denied access to his grandeur?"

An ugly, misshapen creature stood in the doorway, still hurling anathemas over his shoulder at the unfortunate Grisar, whom he had sent sprawling across the room with a vigorous play of his elbow. Now he hobbled forward on one leg and a wooden stump, with which he banged the floor until it shivered and shook, as without further ceremony he entered the inner sanctum of Citizen Commissary Bossut.

Grisar had in the meanwhile sufficiently recovered his balance to call for assistance from the men on duty, when the newcomer once more raised his raucous voice. But this time he neither sore nor stormed. His ugly face became distorted with an ugly leer; he put a grimy finger up to his very red nose and winked--yes, winked at the commissary himself.

"Do not let those fellows touch me, citizen," he said, "for, if you do, you'll never know what I have come here on purpose to tell you. And," he added, with another knowing wink, "there'll never be another chance of promotion for you as long as you live."

The word promotion acted like magic on Bossut's temper. It was the very breath of life to him: he thought of it all day, he dreamed of it by night. He ordered Grisar and the men out of the room, sat down at his desk, and demanded curtly:

"Well, what is it?"

These being the glorious days of fraternity and equality, the miserable caitiff was not going to allow any commissary to order him about. First, he made himself at home; sat down opposite the commissary; poured out a glass of wine, which he drank down at a gulp. He wiped his mouth with the back of his hand, leaving a wide, sooty streak right across his nose and chin. Finally, he disposed his wooden leg as comfortably as he could, then only was he prepared to speak.

Bossut smothered his wrath, resolved not to lose his temper with a man who had used the magic word, promotion.

"You see, citizen commissary," the man began at last, "it's like this. The Committees have their spies, as you know, and I am one of them. But they are hard task-masters, worse than any tyrant, and you may take it from me that, all in good time, they will be sent to the guillotine. Every one of them--Danton, Hébert, Robespierre--they'll all go presently because--"

"Yes, yes! Never mind about that," the commissary broke in impatiently. "My time is short. Get on with what you have to say."

"All right, all right! I'm coming to it. What I wanted to say was that the Committees demand a lot of work and pay very little for it. I have often brought them information worth the weight of a man's head in gold. You think they would have given me something extra for my pains. Raised my wages. Not a bit of it! I am sick of them. Sick, I tell you. And, what's more, I told them--I told citizen Chauvelin--"

"No wonder that he wouldn't listen to you, my man, you talk too much," Bossut put in, in exasperation.

"He would have liked to know, though, what I alone can tell him about the English spy, the Scarlet Pimpernel."

"What?"

Bossut had jumped to his feet. In a moment his excitement was at fever point. The English spy! The Scarlet Pimpernel! There was no ambitious height to which a man could not reach if he helped in the capture of that poisonous enemy of the Republic.

The cripple contemplated him with a leer upon his ugly face, while Bossut paced up and down the room in order work off his agitation. At last he sat down again, put his elbows on the desk and gazed with concentrated attention on the misshapen creature before him.

"Tell me!" he commanded.

But the other only grinned.

"What'll you pay me for the information?" he asked.

"One half of the reward offered for the capture of the English spy--if I get him."

The caitiff nodded.

"Put that down in writing, citizen commissary," he said, "and the spy is yours. My name's Goujon," he went on--"Amédé Goujon, in the service of the Committees. Put it down in writing, citizen commissary, that you will give me one half of the reward offered for the capture of the Scarlet Pimpernel."

While Bossut, with a hand that shook visibly, put the promise down in writing, signed it and strewed sand over it, the cripple continued to mutter under his breath:

"It'll want pluck. The Englishman is powerful--a giant, what? And cunning! Sacré nom, but he has slipped through Citizen Chauvelin's fingers more than once--just like an eel. Here to-day, gone tomorrow. But there's one man knows just where and how he can be found."

"Tell me!" Bossut commanded.

"Over a bottle of wine, comrade," Goujon declared with a loud guffaw. "Dash it, my friend, my throat is dry. How can I speak?"

Bossut swore, but he went to his locker, produced a fresh bottle of wine with a second mug, and set the wine on the table.

"Now then," he said peremptorily.

"That old fool in the Rue des Pipots," Goujon said in a hoarse whisper, leaning his grimy arms on the table and eagerly watching the commissary as he filled the two mugs with wine, "he who plays about with glass tubes and instruments, eh?"

"Rollin?"

"That's the man."

"But how do you know that Rollin-"

Bossut was so agitated that he could hardly speak.

"I have seen the old fool standing at his window in conversation with the Englishman," Goujon asserted. "Have him arrested, I tell you."

"But I've got him," Bossut exclaimed. "He is in La Roche since this morning."

"Send for him, then," the cripple retorted laconically. "Make him tell you. He knows."

The order was at once given. Grisar and two men were dispatched to the prison of La Roche, not very far distant, with orders to bring along the prisoner, Rollin. Bossut by now was in a state bordering on frenzy, pacing up and down the room like a feline waiting for its food. Goujon, on the other hand, appeared entirely serene. His misshapen body was sprawling on a rickety chair which threatened to break down with every movement of his ungainly body; his wooden leg was stretched out in front of him and he was snorting like a winded nag while he read through, most carefully, the precious paper which the commissary had given him. Satisfied that it was duly dated and signed, he folded it and slipped it into the pocket of his tattered coat, after which he gave himself over to the delight of finishing the commissary's excellent bottle of red wine. He smacked his lips in token of great apprecation.

"Ah!" he said. "It is not often a poor man gets such good wine these days."

Half-an-hour later, Grisar and a couple of men returned with Professor Rollin, who looked more like a scared rabbit than ever. Bossut had resumed his seat behind the desk and Goujon was sprawling between the desk and the prisoner.

"Now then, citizen," the commissary began in his most official tone, "as I told you this morning, you are accused of trafficking with the enemy, notably with your daughter, who is the wife of a traitor and an émigré to boot. What is your answer to that charge?"

"Marguerite," the old man murmured vaguely, blinking his eyes, "my daughter. Yes--a pretty girl But she is not here--and I do not write letters--"

"That is as it may be," the commissary retorted. "But I also happen to know that you traffic not only with an émigré over in England but with the most poisonous enemy of our glorious Revolution, the English spy who is known to our patriotic committees as the Scarlet Pimpernel."

Professor Rollin looked completely bewildered this time. He murmured "Ah," and then again "Ah," and gazed at the commissary over his horn-rimmed spectacles.

"Tell him," Bossut commanded, turning to the crippled loon--"tell him what you saw, Citizen Goujon."

Goujon had drunk a good deal of wine; his speech by now was not very clear.

"I said," he mumbled, "that I saw this old scarecrow at his window in the Rue des Pipots, in conversation with an Englishman who, I say, is none other than that accursed spy who is known as the Scarlet Pimpernel."

"What have you to say to that?" the commissary demanded.

The little Professor had nothing very enlightening to say. He had never heard of the Scarlet Pimpernel and, if he had been seen in conversation with an Englishman, well, that was as it may be. But he certainly didn't know where that Englishman was now. Whereupon Goujon mumbled: "My belief is that if you searched the old scarecrow's nest you would find that cursed spy hidden among the glass tubes."

"No, no!" the Professor hastened to assert. "I assure you, citizen commissary, that you wouldn't find anybody in my laboratory. And--and--I have most valuable instruments there for my experiments. No one must be allowed to touch them--"

"There, now!" Goujon exclaimed triumphantly. "What did I tell you? On the face of it the old fool is lying, as I myself saw the Englishman go into the house in the Rue des Pipots, just before I came on here."

"Why in the devil's name did you not tell me that before?" Bossut exclaimed, bringing a heavy fist crashing down upon the table and nearly upsetting the precious bottle of red wine.

"I did," Goujon asserted imperturbably, "but you were so excited, you did not listen."

The commissary had once more jumped to his feet.

"Citizen Grisar," he demanded, "how many men have we on duty here?"

"Half-a-dozen, citizen."

"Very well. Let these two here remain with the prisoner, and you take the others with you to Number Seventeen, Rue des Pipots, where you were this morning. Search the house through and through. Every apartment, every room, you understand? Make every man, woman and child inside the house show you his card of citizenship, failing which, bring them along here. And do not forget that not only for me, your superior, but for you all there will be a handsome reward if you lay hands on the English spy."

Grisar was keen enough. Indeed, he was only one of many corporals of the National Guard who had seen visions of promotion and good money for the capture of the mysterious Scarlet Pimpernel. The two men who had been ordered to remain on guard over the old scarecrow looked glum, for they were longing to join in the chase. Grisar, on the other hand, had already assembled his small squad and soon they were heard to leave the dingy little building, and their measured tread rang out on the cobblestones of the Rue Monge.

Bossut, who was making vigorous efforts to control his excitement and thus preserving a semblance of dignity before his underlings, resumed his seat and made pretence to busy himself with some papers. From time to time he threw a glance on the prisoner, who stood with long lean hands crossed before him and watery eyes blinking behind his spectacles, his thoughts obviously detached from his surroundings. The two men of the National Guard stood one on each side of him, stolid and unperturbed. Bossut, whose nerves were exacerbated by the constant shifting of their feet upon the creaking floor, curtly ordered the three of them to sit down.

"One more glass, citizen commissary," the cripple said jovially. He had filled the two mugs and drained the bottle of wine to its last drop. Bossut drank, then sat down again to his papers. The air in the narrow room had become overwhelmingly close, with the iron stove roaring and the ceiling lamp sending forth its puffs of evil-smelling odours. Above Bossut's head a white-faced clock ticked with exasperating monotony. But little noise came from outside, only the furtive footsteps of belated passers-by. These were days when it was not good to be abroad after dark. The streets were ill-lighted and Government spies lurked round every corner, stalking likely prey; and one never knew, any chance word lightly uttered might mean summary arrest, with its inevitable awful consequences.

Thus silence and the stuffy atmosphere were equally oppressive. Bossut, despite his excitement, was feeling drowsy. He had great difficulty in keeping his eyes open and his head erect. Now and then he looked up at the clock and then sighed wearily. The cripple was frankly snoring and even the men guarding the prisoner nodded from time to time. Nothing happened, and the minutes passed by leadenfooted. At one moment there was loud noise of altercation in the street. Raucous voices shouting and swearing. Bossut ordered the two soldiers to go and see what it was.

When they returned a few moments later they reported that two street rowdies had come to blows just outside the commissariat, but had already taken to their heels. The commissary himself had, during their short absence, fallen half asleep. They found him still sitting at his desk, but with his head buried in his outstretched arms. He raised his head wearily when the men entered, and cast a bleary glance heavy with sleep upon them. He asked them a question or two in a thick, halting voice, and the next moment his head once more fell on his outstretched arms. Goujon was snoring. Still unperturbed and stolid, the men sat down again on the wooden bench, each side of the prisoner.

Indeed, the latter was the only man here who appeared wide awake and alert. His spectacles had slipped down his nose and from over them his pale, watery eyes wandered from one face to the other with a kind of vaguely-scared expression.

And all at once it seemed as if a tornado had burst into the room for, with a crash of broken glass, the lamp was suddenly extinguished. There was a bang and a groan, and then a call: "A moi!" followed by quick, light footsteps hurrying into the room from outside. The soldiers had jumped to their feet, grasping their muskets. But the place was now in pitch darkness and, before the two of them could even in a small measure collect their senses together, heavy cloths were thrown over their heads and wound tightly over their mouths and eyes. The muskets were taken out of their hands, their arms were tied behind their backs and their legs pinioned with cords to the wooden bench on which they were forced to sit down--all in the space of three minutes. Through the cloth over their heads they heard muffled sounds of words they did not understand, but which one of them afterwards declared was English. Then there was more tramping of feet, and finally silence. The men could not move. They could hardly breathe. Soon they lost consciousness.

When, an hour or so later, Grisar and his small squad returned from their long and fruitless errand, after they had scoured the house in the Rue des Pipots from attic to cellar and found no trace of any English spy, they were appalled at the sight which met their gaze. To begin with, the two rooms of the commissariat were in complete darkness. That was astonishing enough, and a light was soon struck. But it was the sight of the commissary's inner sanctum that was so appalling. The commissary himself was sprawling across his desk in an obvious state of collapse. To the wooden bench facing the desk the two soldiers of the National Guard, comrades of Grisar, were securely tied with ropes, their heads muffled in clothes, their hands tied behind their backs. Bits of glass littered the desk and the floor, a chair was overturned, and the ceiling lamp hung crooked from a single chain, the others being broken. But the strangest sight of all was that a wooden stump, such as were used by indigent cripples who had lost a leg, was lying on the floor, with its leather straps cut, and in a confused mass of rags and cloth of every description.

What in the world had happened? Grisar set his men to free their comrades, to get them water and wine and generally to try to restore them to consciousness, while he himself busied himself with the person of his chief. After a time, all three came to, but when questioned, not one of them knew exactly what had happened. Bossut was not yet free of his drugged sleep, during which, apparently, he had been hit violently on the head, which ached furiously. He knew nothing save that a cripple named Goujon had visited him and had induced him to send his subordinate and a small squad to search a certain house in the Rue des Pipots, where the prisoner, Rollin, was supposed to have held converse with the noted English spy known as the Scarlet Pimpernel. By the way, where in the devil's name was the prisoner, Rollin? Bossut remembered seeing him sitting quietly on the wooden bench between the guard, and giving no trouble. He also remembered the guard leaving the premises in order to ascertain what the noise of an altercation in the street was about. But after that, complete oblivion clouded his brain. Nor could the soldiers give any more lucid explanation of the mysterious affair. One or two facts that certainly were strange they did recall, namely, that after they had been out in the street and seen the street rowdies take to their heels, they had noticed that the light in the room was very dim and that the citizen commissary seemed to be in an extraordinary state of somnolence. The breaking of the lamp and the attack made on them in the dark had been so sudden that their impression of it all was of the vaguest.

The matter had to be left at that for the moment. All six men who had more or less suffered through the affair remained convinced that the English spy was in one manner or other responsible for it. Although, as he and his henchmen were known to be real aristos of imposing mien and luxuriously dressed, it was difficult to determine what rôle the crippled caitiff, Goujon, played in the drama, and why he had been so cruelly deprived of his wooden leg.

Since neither the English spies nor the prisoner, Rollin, were possessed of identity papers, it would be impossible for them to leave Paris, and their recapture was only a matter of time.

III

It was some three of four days later that the guard at the north-west gate challenged a carrier who, in addition to two passengers, had three large crates under the hood of his cart. The crates were labelled "candles" and the bill of lading which the carrier presented declared the goods to have been manufactured by the firm of Turandot, of Paris. The passports and identity of the three men appeared to be in perfect order, signed and countersigned by the Commissary of the section and the chief commissary of the district, but as Citizen Lebrun had been specially warned--along with the guard of every gate in Paris--to be on the look-out for three fugitives of enemy nationality and an escaped prisoner named Rollin, all of whom would presumably be armed with forged passports, he had for the past three days been more than usually careful in examining all identity papers presented to him. Although the carrier and his two companions appeared harmless enough, he was none the less careful this time. He took their papers from them and ordered the three men to alight. Moreover, the ordered the three crates to be taken down from the cart and opened so that he might satisfy himself that no escaped prisoner was hidden among the candles.

The carrier protested as vigorously as he dared. He and his two sons, he declared, were honest citizens and would know how to avenge this insult that was being put upon them. As for the candles, they were a consignment which he had to deliver to a grocer at Meaux.

Lebrun, undaunted by threats, stood by with the papers in his hand, superintending the opening of the crates, when there came riding from the city a mounted squad of the National Guard, with an officer in command. Lebrun was quite thankful to see them. The officer could but commend him for his zeal and relieve him of ultimate responsibility.

The small squad drew rein and the officer, in response to Sergeant Lebrun's salute, asked him the meaning of the empty cart, the broken crates and the three wildly-gesticulating citizens.

"You have done well, citizen sergeant," the officer said as soon as Lebrun had put him in possession of the facts, "and the authorities shall hear of your zeal. Let's have a look at those papers," he went on, "and also at this mysterious cart."

Lebrun handed him the papers and could not help noting that he frowned in obvious doubt and suspicion while he scanned the signatures upon them.

"You had better write out your report at once and I myself will take it to the proper quarters. This is a very curious and a serious case Silence!" he thundered, for the carrier and his two sons had again begun to protest vigorously. "Citizen sergeant, have them taken into the guardroom with you. I want to have a closer look at this mysterious cart."

Lebrun then turned into the guardroom, taking the three civilians and one or two of his men with him. The broken crates remained out in the road, as did the cart, round which the mounted squad had now assembled. The guard of the gate stood by at attention.

And suddenly there was a quick word of command, "En avant! Bride abattue!" which means, "Hell for leather!" and the whole squad, led by their officer, thundered past the bewildered guard through the gate and up the country road which leads straight as an arrow to the north.

The noise had brought Sergeant Lebrun out of the guardroom. Half-a-dozen excited and confused voices told him what had happened.

"They seemed to be examining the cart--"

"And then suddenly--"

"They were gone--"

"It was like a thunder-clap--

"And a flash of lightning--"

"Stay!" Lebrun thundered loudly through the din. "Was the gate open?"

"Why, yes, citizen sergeant," one of the men said. "It was opened at nine o'clock, as usual. You were there when--"

"Did nothing happen just before they rode away?"

"Nothing, citizen sergeant. They were all round the cart and suddenly they rode away."

"Well, I suppose," Lebrun said slowly, "that they had their orders."

He felt bewildered and was vaguely anxious. He had heard tales--but no, no, of course it could not be!--tales of English spies--surely they were old wives' tales!

"I suppose they really were troopers of the National Guard?" one of the men suggested.

"Name of a dog!" remarked another. "I remember now--"

"What?" Lebrun demanded shakily.

"That one of the troopers had another riding pillion behind him."

"A smallish man," he added. "I didn't see his face, but he didn't look at home in the saddle. I thought he was a recruit--or a deserter, may be, poor devil. One often sees them these days. A youngster, probably, for he was small and thin. And, anyway, it was not my place to ask questions."

Lebrun by now was in a state of collapse. What the whole thing meant he couldn't say; what he should do now was more bewildering still. It took time before his men had reported at headquarters and a squad of genuine National Guard got to horse and went in pursuit. But of the other squad who had a smallish man with them riding pillion behind one of the troopers there was no longer a trace upon the great north road which runs straight to the sea.

Vatour, the carrier, and his two sons always declared that the episode was a punishment on Sergeant Lebrun for the insult which he had put on those three honest patriots.

As for professor Rollin, he never knew exactly what happened to him after he found himself summarily lifted off the wooden bench in the dingy room of the commissariat of police. For three days he had lived in a dank and disused cellar, waited on by his English friend. Then there were days when he was hoisted into a saddle and ordered to cling to the rider in front of him, which he did with a strength born of despair; days which he spent in the open, in forest or cavern; an awful day when he was very seasick on an English ship; and finally there was the happy day when he was delivered like a limp bundle of goods into the arms of his loving daughter in London. Bruised in body, but not in spirit, he returned with zest to his experiments, and, I believe it to be a fact that in due time he had a personal interview with the great Jenner himself.

THE END

Also from Benediction Books ...

Wandering Between Two Worlds: Essays on Faith and Art
Anita Mathias
Benediction Books, 2007
152 pages
ISBN: 0955373700

Available from www.amazon.com, www.amazon.co.uk

In these wide-ranging lyrical essays, Anita Mathias writes, in lush, lovely prose, of her naughty Catholic childhood in Jamshedpur, India; her large, eccentric family in Mangalore, a sea-coast town converted by the Portuguese in the sixteenth century; her rebellion and atheism as a teenager in her Himalayan boarding school, run by German missionary nuns, St. Mary's Convent, Nainital; and her abrupt religious conversion after which she entered Mother Teresa's convent in Calcutta as a novice. Later rich, elegant essays explore the dualities of her life as a writer, mother, and Christian in the United States-- Domesticity and Art, Writing and Prayer, and the experience of being "an alien and stranger" as an immigrant in America, sensing the need for roots.

About the Author

Anita Mathias is the author of *Wandering Between Two Worlds: Essays on Faith and Art.* She has a B.A. and M.A. in English from Somerville College, Oxford University, and an M.A. in Creative Writing from the Ohio State University, USA. Anita won a National Endowment of the Arts fellowship in Creative Nonfiction in 1997. She lives in Oxford, England with her husband, Roy, and her daughters, Zoe and Irene.

Visit Anita's website
http://www.anitamathias.com,
and Anita's blog
http://dreamingbeneaththespires.blogspot.com, (Dreaming Beneath the Spires).

The Church That Had Too Much
Anita Mathias
Benediction Books, 2010
52 pages
ISBN: 9781849026567

Available from www.amazon.com, www.amazon.co.uk

The Church That Had Too Much was very well-intentioned. She wanted to love God, she wanted to love people, but she was both hampered by her muchness and the abundance of her possessions, and beset by ambition, power struggles and snobbery. Read about the surprising way The Church That Had Too Much began to resolve her problems in this deceptively simple and enchanting fable.

About the Author

Anita Mathias is the author of *Wandering Between Two Worlds: Essays on Faith and Art.* She has a B.A. and M.A. in English from Somerville College, Oxford University, and an M.A. in Creative Writing from the Ohio State University, USA. Anita won a National Endowment of the Arts fellowship in Creative Nonfiction in 1997. She lives in Oxford, England with her husband, Roy, and her daughters, Zoe and Irene.

Visit Anita's website
http://www.anitamathias.com,
and Anita's blog
http://dreamingbeneaththespires.blogspot.com (Dreaming Beneath the Spires).

www.ingramcontent.com/pod-product-compliance
Lightning Source LLC
Chambersburg PA
CBHW030343310726
48979CB00001B/171
9781849023467